Chang Ying-Tai is a Taiwanese writer and Professor at National Taiwan University of Science and Technology. She holds a PhD in Literature from National Taiwan University. Over the past decade, her writing has garnered numerous accolades, including *China Times Prize for Literature*, *United Daily News Literature Prize*, *Taiwan Literature Award* and *Lennox Robinson Literary Award*.

The Bear Whispers to Me is her first book to be translated into English.

Darryl Sterk has translated numerous short stories by Taiwanese writers for *The Taipei Chinese Pen*, *Asymptote* and *Pathlight*. His first novel translation is Wu Ming-Yi's *The Man with the Compound Eyes*. He teaches translation in the Graduate Program at National Taiwan University.

As a scholar he works on the representation of Taiwan's indigenous peoples in film and fiction.

CHANG YING-TAI

The Bear Whispers to Me

The Story of a Bear and a Boy

Translated from the Chinese
by Darryl Sterk

balestierpress

Balestier Press
71-75 Shelton Street, London WC2H 9JQ
www.balestier.com

The Bear Whispers to Me
Original title: 熊兒悄聲對我說
Copyright © Chang Ying-Tai, 2007
English translation copyright © Darryl Sterk, 2015

Songs on pages 11, 50, 67, 114, 115, 116, and 171 are from
the folk songs of Hla'alua, an aboriginal tribe of Taiwan.

First published in English by Balestier Press in 2015

ISBN 978 0 9932154 0 7

The Bear Whispers to Me

The Story of a Bear and a Boy

Prologue
Page Turning

Our tribe was fashioned by the Celestial Spirit from the leaves of every tree.
—A sample of Father's cramped handwriting

At the time he wrote this, he was carefully recording everything that had happened in the mountains.

He didn't tell me what he was doing; it was like he was keeping secrets. I only started finding out about Father's secrets the year I turned twelve, when I came across a proverb in a scrapbook that Father had started when he was ten years old. Father never ever told me stories or bought me children's storybooks. I had only a single pastime to relieve the loneliness of my childhood: to take Father's keys and open up all of his drawers, feeling a bit like a thief, or maybe like a sleuth. I found a scrapbook in one of the drawers. It was wrapped in brown kraft paper and pressed under a rusted metal box. In the box, Father had stored a pair of delicate bird's nests. One was shaped like a bowl and woven out of bits of bark, grass, moss and lichen. The other was spherical, with an entrance on the side. Holding the latter up to the lamp, I saw that the interior seemed to be made of dry bamboo leaves and silver grass, with very fine down crammed in the cracks. A few filaments of this down had been pressed between two of the pages of the scrapbook for so long they had become stuck to one of the pages. On the opposite page was a drawing of a little bird. I would stare at this little bird, wondering if it was the one to which the down belonged. I just have to find out what kind of bird this is, I often thought, like it was a lead I'd been pursuing for too long to just give up and let it be.

Later on I made myself a drawer with a lock and key, like I too had secrets to keep, like I finally had my own story to tell. But the first story I collected came from Father.

The proverb in the scrapbook seems exotic:

When a needle falls in the forest, the eagle sees it, the deer hears it and the bear smells it. The eagle, deer and bear are the eyes, ears and nose of the Celestial Spirit.

He must have been about ten when he wrote this proverb. I don't know why he copied out this particular one. Or why he failed to finish filling the scrapbook. Except for bits of fluff and little drawings of birds and insects, it had nothing much to tell me. For some reason, he copied this proverb out and left the rest of the scrapbook mostly blank.

It wasn't until I found the key to a certain cabinet, which to me at the time seemed like a veritable treasure chest, that I was able to continue my sleuthing career. Inside the cabinet I found an album. This album contained no foreign proverb to arouse my curiosity, only a series of crayon drawings with explanatory captions. It was an album, but it was also like a diary; the captioned illustrations were like diary entries. Father dated each of the entries, and, based on the dates, he must have been twelve years old when he completed his diary-album.

This is the caption for the first picture in the album:

Our tribe was fashioned by the Celestial Spirit from the leaves of every tree. After we die our spirits fly, guided by the light of the moon up to the highest peak.

The picture itself is of a darkling forest with the moon and a constellation of stars shining brilliantly overhead. There is a clearing in the forest, and a cabin with a lattice window in the clearing. There is no sense of wind. But somehow when I gazed at the picture as a twelve year old child, it seemed to come alive. The leaves would start falling from the trees and twirling in the breeze. I could make out the veins in the leaves, which would transform into jingling musical notes as they floated down through the moonlight and starlight towards the cabin. Through the lattice window I could make out a children's storybook set upon a table, open to the very first page. Then, in a close-up, I would see the proverb from Father's scrapbook:

When a needle falls in the forest, the eagle sees it, the deer hears it and the bear smells it. They are the eyes, ears and nose of the Celestial Spirit.

The page would turn and I would see a pine tree and a pine needle hanging in midair beneath a branch. I would stare and stare, and the pages of the storybook would turn and turn, showing me an eagle, eyes wide open, perched on a branch, a deer with its ears cocked, and a bear poking its head out of a cave.

The second picture in Father's album adopts a different perspective: it lets you see the world from inside the cabin. The storybook is still on the table, but now you see a gigantic scarab beetle sharing the tabletop. It must be a pet scarab, because there is a string tied in a loop around its neck. The scarab is shiny blue and black, and its head is buried in a rotten peach. The peach is brownish, except for a pink ripe-and-juicy part, which the scarab would polish off in a single bite. The other end of the string is held by a boy—that must be Father—who would have to hold his pet scarab back when it would attempt to crawl out through an opening in the lattice window. Through the window a faint breeze would blow in bits of flashing dandelion fluff. The boy would put his mouth near and the spores would scatter, some floating back up to become twinkling stars in the night-time sky, others floating towards the marsh and turning into glowworms. Two of the glowworms would drift into a mountain cave, looking just like a pair of eyes, round and bright, staring right at you. Here Father wrote a second caption:

In the whole wide world, apart from that pair of eyes glowing in the mountain cave, I have no one to watch over me.

The breeze would blow and blow, turning the pages of the storybook on the table by the lattice window, until the last page would flip shut. At that moment, the constellation of stars, and the moon itself, would shine all the brighter through the lattice window of the cabin in the woods, into my father's childhood world. The moon and the stars keep shining and shining, like insomniac eyes, like silent deathless spirits.

But it seems there were many things to listen to in Father's world. He recorded many sounds in the album he buried in the ground.

One is a light throaty sound, *gulooo gulooo gulooo ...*

Another is a quick sound produced in the depths of the belly, *guh guh guh guh guh guh...*

There's also a whistling sound, *shhhhhiuuuu, shhhhhiuuuuu...*

There's even a song in Father's album! When I first saw the lyrics to this ancient tribal song, I tried to read them, but found them unintelligible:

nasicui rumahlaree rumaihlaveesa
ihlaveesa imiravusa vulahla
vulahla ui hlalumalumai
hlalumalumai hlimahlulailai 'ampulai laita iaiaai

To you, too, it may seem that these lines are simply gobbledygook. But I promise you, they are the lyrics of a sacred song written in a language that people once used to share their memories, and that people still use when they talk in their dreams.

And it may seem to you that the pictures in his album, too, are made up, silly childhood fantasies. But I assure you, the events in the pictures really happened. I know, because I have become intimately familiar with the places in the pictures—I have come to know every kind of tree and bush, every sound and smell. I have visited these hills, this secluded little corner of the world. Its history is lost, unrecorded and untraceable. Except for this album, there is no proof, not even any evidence. There is really very little to go on. But together the pictures in the album tell a coherent story, the story of a boy and a bear. And this story really happened. You must believe me: Father would not lie!

Father's album brings you to a roadside field of ripe beans. Imagine white and purple flowers. You can almost see them nodding in the breeze. You smell sweet mountain berries and the odour of dirt moistened by dew and you start walking along a path. You walk and walk, until the path crosses a steep slope. It is high summer. Spring water trickles down the slope. A cloud of butterflies flutter over to drink. Several hundred pairs of fanning wings paint a swathe of brilliant colour in midair. The path forks, one route leading down into a narrow gully, dark and cool, haunted by ladybirds, scarab beetles, crickets, grasshoppers and praying mantises. Instead of going down the gully, you keep going straight, until the path finally ends at a primeval forest. In the forest, there is a thick carpet of fallen leaves, through which cimicids and centipedes crawl. You choose a spot and use your foot to brush away the layer of leaves, revealing stag beetles and rhinoceros beetles creeping around on the moist soil. Clearing away the soil, you uncover a colony of hister beetles gnawing on the putrid corpse of a rat. In a couple of decaying tree stumps, you find shiny black longhorn beetles and click bugs going at the rotten wood like there is no tomorrow. By the stumps is an animal dropping and, on a patch of ground next to the faeces, the stench of urine. A single dung beetle, knowing it can't finish off the dropping in a single meal, is rolling it towards its lair. The urine attracts several cabbage whites and leaf butterflies, which pause here to mud-puddle.

You keep going through the forest until you come to a clearing, at the foot of another slope. The clearing looks somehow familiar. You see a cabin—my father's cabin. In front of the window of the cabin, a couple of leaves twirl in midair. Looking more closely, you see a fuzzy bee transporting the leaves. The leaves disappear into the bamboo pole on which Father used to dry his clothes. You split the bamboo and find hidden inside what look like swaddling clothes, but are actually insect eggs wrapped in leaves that have been shaped into cones. Some grubs have already hatched from the eggs in the cones, and some of the grubs are already mature. They are getting ready to pupate.

After dark, the mists have blanched the hills. Extending up from the cabin for miles, all the way to the crest of the mountain, is a belt of pines, a sea of green. Into this sea a goshawk suddenly dives. When it bottoms out and rises again, there is a large lizard squirming in its claws.

yike-Yiiiike yike-Yiiiike is its triumphant call.

The sounds are clearly indicated in speech bubbles in the pictures. I tried to imitate the sound of a goshawk by whistling, but it came out sounding like the *yieeoou-yieeoou* of a streak-throated fulvetta, not the majestic and desolate cry of a hawk. Way above, in the upper reaches of a canyon, a crested serpent eagle perches next to its nest on a branch of a craggy tree. It is regurgitating bits of snake meat and feeding them to its young. *Who-you-who-you hooo hooo* is its sure and resonant call. A huge eagle comes round a ridge and, flying low, takes sight of a hare. It blows its cover too early, though, and his prey eludes it; but then it spots a fawn caught in a hunter's trap, easy pickings for the eagle, which is so intent on devouring the deer that you no longer hear its calm, confident call. But just then the silence is broken by a white-bellied green pigeon cooing *oooowa-oooowa*, forming a creepy accompaniment to the sound of the eagle feeding.

In the moonlight, the silver branches of the pines seem covered in tiny blue buds, and on one branch rests a scimitar babbler with a long, black eye-stripe: *kwa-kway-kway*.

On another branch is a pair of songbirds: *gwo-gogo... gwo-gogo... gwo-gogo*.

And a delicate, perfectly round grey-headed thrush perches on a third branch: *jeeeep jeep jeep jeep, jeeeep jeep jeep jeep*. (Here Father noted: A light nasal sound.)

Then the sweetest little thing comes leaping over a

thicket of grass. It has a copper neck and an olive body. It hops along vines heavy with tomatoes and scurries into another tuft of grass. Its call is *chiu-chi, chiu-chi, cho cho cho cho*.

What's that? Father asks an old man by his side wearing a buckskin hat and a black sleeveless sweater.

Red-headed thrush, the old man says.

At the tip of a soaring tree is another little creature, this one white-crested and black-cheeked.

Teechee, teechee, it says.

It's a black chickadee, says the old man.

What about that skinny bird in the silver grass calling teecha teecha? asks Father.

Brown hill-warbler.

The old man has a pouch slung round his neck and a curved knife at his hip. His body glows. The moonlight casts his shadow on the ground. It is the shadow of a massive beast.

Father calls him *Grandpa*.

Father's grandfather only appears in human form on this night, on this page of the album. But he is in other pictures, too, as a ray of light, a gust of wind, a leaf or a glimmering moonshadow.

Father understood birdsong, almost certainly taught to him by his grandfather. The old songs Father recorded were probably taught to him by his grandfather, too, along with natural and ritual lore.

On one page Father adopted his grandfather's tone and wrote about how our tribe once lived in the north at Hlaseng, a place we shared with a population of dwarf spirits. Our people got along really well with the dwarf spirits, so well that when we left Hlaseng, the dwarf spirits gave us twelve Sacred Shells, which we handed down to generation after generation. These shells were preternatural, capable of invisibility, shapeshifting and flight. Every year at our tribe's biggest ritual we would worship the shells, praying for protection and abundance. The ritual was always held after the millet harvest.

When I was twelve years old, I made a small hut by our house out of twitch grass, rattan and green bamboo, just like the Forbidden Room that Father drew on one page of his album. I placed sacred objects inside a rectangular box, a shrine made of tough old vines and arrow bamboo, just like in Father's album. Father used to call this box the Holy Vault.

I also made a house for hunters which I called the Lodge of Braves. It was a bamboo platform raised three feet above the ground, and it had an awning. Beneath it was a pile of firewood. Inside were long racks constructed out of the bones of beasts. On the racks were trophies of the hunt: ram skulls, boar tusks and deer antlers. Also hung on the wall was all the equipment a warrior could ever need: a hunting knife, pike, spear, bow and arrow, buckskin cap, tunic, quiver and pouch. I was too young to have my own hunting gear, much less my own trophies. But I could certainly draw and colour these things on cardboard and cut them out to hang on the wall of the Lodge of Braves. It was like an inventory of antique curiosities, or talismans protecting the hunt.

What animals did Father hunt? In his album, on page

after page, he recorded wolves, boars, squirrels, muntjacs, leopards, rattlesnakes and bears, especially bears. I sometimes wonder whether Father really saw all of these creatures, let alone hunted them.

For as a child Father was thin and weak and easily scared. A man used to cook praying mantis eggs, or grind the dried bodies of mantises into powder, for Father to eat. Hill folk in those days apparently believed that cooked mantis eggs cured bedwetting, while the powder was a remedy for the colic. This man had a gloomy face, like a tired old tree bound tight by tendrils and creepers. He was my grandfather, my father's father. Father rarely called him Father. Usually he called him Momo, or Moe for short.

The year I was twelve, I found the keys to my father's drawers as well as his cabinet. I found two books he'd made, a scrapbook and an album, and followed the hints they contained back into his childhood. Father never gave me a storybook to read. While I was growing up, I lived in a world of my own. All I had were his stories. I planned to write stories of my own, partly real, partly make-believe, and put them in a storybook. But the first story I ever wrote was Father's. I walked step by step, page by page, back into the alpine world in Father's album. I intended to keep walking day after day, month after month, year after year, until one day I wouldn't have to wander any more. Then I would return, exhausted, to that cabin in the clearing in the woods. I was sure there would be a stool waiting there just for me, and a steaming pot of rice porridge on the stove, along with a book of stories of our family—Father, Grandfather Momo, Great-grandfather, and me—the stories of our tribe, the pages turning one by one in the wind. Then the wind would die down. In that moment of perfect tranquillity, I hoped that, though I might be alone, I would no longer be lonely.

Not everything a boy hopes for can come true. But at least now there is an intelligible written record—you hold it in your hands—of the world Father once knew.

This is how I've told the story of Father's childhood.

1

A Boy's Book of Bears

I live past the outskirts of a remote mountain village. Every day, the moon rises and sets. The rising moon has a living face. The setting moon is a mask of death. Grandpa says that all the world's departed spirits are blown by the night breeze up towards the moon, which sets them in the night sky. The moon takes them with it when it sets, and brings them back when it rises again the next night. So if you want a ghost to keep you company, you need to wait until it gets dark.

The moonlight is like a demon. It turns the trees black, shining only on a silvery shell at the base of a slope. That silvery shell is the cabin I live in. It is located at the foot of a mountain, a good hike from the village, so far that when you're inside you can't hear anyone. You feel as if the nearest person could be a thousand miles away. There are wild animals around, of course, which is why the cabin has a protective palisade, a fence made of bamboo posts.

In my palisaded cabin in the hills, I rarely hear a human voice. I listen to the wind through the trees and the bird and insect calls, and that's about it. But I do have at least one person to listen to, a storyteller named Momo. Momo is my special name for my father. I've occasionally heard folks calling him Moe, or "Moe my man". So I started calling him Moe too. First Moe, then Momo. Momo sounds more affectionate than plain old "Father" or "Dad", and he doesn't seem to mind. Though he doesn't let me call him Momo in front of other people. Maybe he thinks it sounds silly.

The story Momo used to read to me was in a storybook he bought me one time on a visit to the big city. At first, I couldn't read the words in the book, which was all right, because Momo would explain the pictures. "This is a Formosan white collar bear. This is an Indian sloth bear. This is a grizzly bear, a polar bear, a bear making its lair in a tree, a bear eating honey…" Actually, there are many animals in the book and not very many bears. But for some reason the bears strike my fancy. The story itself is short; there are not actually that many pictures. Day after day, Momo's explanations got more and more predictable, as monotonous as life in the mountains, yet they never became tedious. Even if at times Momo's storytelling was just a little bit dull, I still kept listening, as there would usually be a few lively expressions. Sometimes Momo lost his patience and only continued if I promised to be a good boy—only then would he tell the story all the way to the end, though he would shorten it a bit, especially if he thought it was time for me to go to bed.

Later he wanted me to learn to read and refused to tell me the story. He seemed less and less like Momo and more like a stern Father. I went off the book that had once enthralled me so. I didn't want to read the story on my own. Instead I started drawing pictures of bears on the blank pages at the end of the storybook. At first all the bears looked the same. But gradually, each bear came to have its own unique appearance, lifestyle, personality and story.

The first bear I drew by copying the bear pelt hanging on the wall—it is the only decoration and also the most precious thing we have in the cabin. The pelt is almost complete: even the head, ears, nose and eyes are there. The only parts that don't match the rest are the amber glass eyes, which have a cunning and harsh expression. But if you get really close, the harshness changes into a sense of ancient mystery.

Every morning at dawn, when Momo shoulders his load and goes out to work, I am supposed to dust the pelt. There isn't really anything to do. It is always already clean and even glossy. Every evening before going to bed, Father gives it another tidying, so I don't really need to do anything. What a chore! Sometimes, secretly, I don't bother. Instead, I cuddle up to the pelt, stroke its thick fur and think up a story. The pelt seems like an old friend or a family member, someone old and wise like a grandparent. Yes, this bear is probably hard of hearing and full of years.

You're probably thinking that Momo's a hunter, but that's not how the bear pelt came into our family. Momo used to work in a lumber mill. One time when they were sawing up a massive tree trunk, they found a bear sleeping in a hollow inside. Flabbergasted, Father and his workmates killed it. They could not understand why the sound of the sawing had not woken it up. Do bears really sleep like the dead when they hibernate? It was too bad for the bear, but they just couldn't take a chance. It might have woken up and eaten them.

"It was either it or us." That's what Father said.

They divvied up the liver, paws and meat and sold the bushmeat on consignment at a mountain produce store, making a tidy sum. The only thing Father kept for himself was the pelt, as a memento. Not long after, Father hurt his leg and had to quit the job at the mill. Mother was very sick at the time, so he stayed at home and cared for her. There was a time when the firewood and rice ran out, but Father would not leave to go and sell the pelt. Only after Mother died did Father get another job. He started selling breadmen, which are a bit like gingerbread men but made out of glutinous rice flour. He carries his stand and his wares on his back when he goes out in the morning.

Morning! I hear Father get up and putter around the house. He closes the old wooden door softly behind him when he leaves. He limps slowly in his cloth shoes across the gravel yard, opens the creaky gate in the bamboo palisade and closes it behind him, replacing the latch before setting off. I squint through the crack at the bottom of the lattice window, but I can't see anything moving outside. I sleep in for a while, not really sleeping, mind you, just pretending to sleep. I always do this, because I have to listen for any sign of Father returning. He might sneak back, you know, and peer in at me—to check on me, to be sure I stay at home and don't go out and get into trouble. His footsteps finally vanish in the distance. I jump out of bed and start planning where I will go today. It's Sunday! There is still some hot rice porridge on the stove. I carry my special magnolia wood stool over to the stove and eat the porridge.

After breakfast, I go out to rinse my mouth and clean the pots and pans in the mountain stream that flows down the slope behind the cabin. Then, ladle by ladle, I fill up the cistern with water from the stream. Those are all my chores. The rest of the day is mine!

Though there is not really that much time in a day, it is sometimes hard to think up things to do. I clean up a bit, but there's not much to clean: just two old beds, a table, an old-fashioned stone stove, and a spider's web, which I can never bring myself to break. Soon, at the most ten days, a mosquito or bug will get caught in the web. I want to see what the spider will do with it. But there has been no sign of the spider for a long time. I am taking care of his web for him, as if it's me that has spun it, as if I am guarding my own web.

Below the base of the wall lives a snail. I have been watching over him for quite some time now. I tease him until he extends his two eyestalks and feelers, and give him fresh mountain greens to eat. When he creeps onto the leaves and begins nibbling away, he leaves a slimy milky trail, which I like to wipe with my finger. But sometimes, irritatingly, he refuses to budge, just hides inside his shell.

There are no other children living nearby. The only friend I have in the yard outside is a rooster we keep cooped up. But he is not long for this world. Father says once he fattens up a little we'll wring his neck and make a nourishing stew out of him. The rooster was bought especially for me. Father says I'm too thin and need nourishment. But so what? I'm going to lose one of my only sources of fun. Even if it does get repetitive, I like to watch Rooster rushing about everywhere in search of insects.

I am in fact myself an expert critter-catcher. I pluck a thorn from a cluster of flowers, find an old tree and stab the thorn into the crevices and hollows. Impaled on the thorn when I pull it out is a line of fat little white bugs.

Being able to eat so many bugs all at once makes Rooster very happy. Full up, he has to play with me. The way we play is simple: I toss pebbles at his rear end, and he clucks and runs away. If I throw hard enough he flaps up onto the roof.

Once up, he doesn't dare come down. He just races around up there.

Playing cat and mouse with a rooster on the roof is more fun than on the ground. He is a wimp, fat and lazy. On the ground he often gives himself up for capture. But on the roof he plays in earnest, fleeing for dear life.

By the time he is too tired to run any more, I am tired of chasing him too. He acknowledges defeat and collapses into my lap, letting me hold him like a pet dog or cat.

With that fat rooster in my lap, I find a shady spot on

the ridge of the roof, enjoying the breeze and watching the sun peek now and then through the clouds. Bugs buzz by my ear, birds call in the air. Sometimes I flip through the storybook if I have brought it up with me. Today I'll just close my eyes and zone out—there can't be anywhere in the world more free-and-easy than here. But then I am roused by a sound, one that seems extremely familiar. I look around but can't see anything that could be making the sound. I know it can't be far off, though—from the roof, even the peak in the distance looks pretty near.

Yes, it would not be too far for me to walk.

I slip down, let Rooster go and enter the Lodge of Braves to get some gear together. When I come out, I rearrange the straw behind me, so nobody can tell that there's a hidden hunter's hut behind our house.

Today I've brought a water gun and a large black umbrella. This might be a long journey. I'd better get some rice, salt and a small axe. Fully equipped, I fit the gate latch and start along that old familiar way.

This path is a secret route I discovered last year. From behind the house, I follow the stream along the slope, around the arc of a jutting precipice, on and on, until the way seems to end at a grove of moso bamboo. After cutting through the grove, I come to the pile of stones I made to remind myself to turn right. A hop, skip and jump and I am clambering along a ramshackle planked walkway, an old corduroy road. The road leads me to another grove, this one full of moss and mushrooms. This is my shortcut up the mountain.

2
A Solitary Encounter

It is so quiet here in this mountain grove, with nothing to disturb you. Occasionally there is a kind of whispering warbling, almost like the wind rustling through the leaves. Looking up, I see some beautiful forms darting through the trees, a red-headed chickadee perhaps, and maybe a goldenwing thrush, a green-backed chickadee and a Swinhoe's thicket flycatcher. Then there's the drone of what must be a huge cicada. A monotonous melody, it seems like the only noise in the forest.

And monotonous is another kind of quiet.

I stop and listen. Each sound is so deep and clear. A beam of light washes down. I squint up at the tops of the trees, listening intently.

It's a light *cheep cheep jeep-jeep-jeep, cheep cheep jeep-jeep*.

"Red-headed chickadee," say I. A grand yet desolate whistle. "White-whiskered laughingthrush." A piercing *meeee–doray–meeee*.

I can't tell. *White-tailed robin*, Grandpa fills in.

koo koo–koo, Koo Koo–Koo, more and more insistently.

Ho ho, a lesser coucal, Grandpa says.

The wind keeps blowing through our hair, a comfortable and peaceful feeling, like being petted by a pair of fleshy hands. Grandpa tells me to memorize the bird calls he has just taught me.

I say I have.

I am still standing in the breeze, enjoying its caress. Then I hear the sound of footsteps approaching slowly, but not too near. I open my eyes: a beekeeper is passing through the woods with a hive on his back. He gives me a look, as if he is used to giving me a friendly nod every time he passes by.

"Hey, kid! You by yourself?"

I've seen him twice before. But this is the first time he's spoken to me. I don't think I need to reply properly, as the man is probably just being nice. Expressionless, I watch him leave. I nod at him, but probably he doesn't see. Soon he is gone.

I climb up a big tree, to where there is a delicate little bowl-shaped nest that seems to be woven out of fine spears of grass, moss, lichen and stalks of silver grass. Inside there are four milky eggs with a lot of tiny purplish-brown spots on one end. I break off a twig and prod them.

"What kind of bird is this?"

Rufous-cheeked laughingthrush, says an aged voice, blown on the wind.

I climb another tree, and high up off the ground find another bowl-shaped nest, built from dried tree and bamboo leaves, containing eggs with tawny freckles.

"What's this one?"

Yellow chickadee, a voice in my head answers.

Climbing along the branch, I find a spherical nest made from silver grass, dried bamboo leaves and down. Peering in the opening on the side, I see copper coloured eggs inside.

"This one?"

Yellow-bellied bush warbler.

I slip down to a lower branch and find a nest made only out of twigs. In the nest are milky coloured eggs without any markings.

Emerald dove. The voice is right by my ear.

Descending to the clump of grass at the base of the tree, I discover another nest, built from dried leaves and grass. Inside which are several eggs with light yellow and russet spots.

"Rufous-cheeked laughingthrush." This was my own voice, though Grandpa had put the name on my tongue.

Over and over again, I review my newfound knowledge, taking out the willow whistle from my pocket and trying to play the calls one by one.

This whistle is Momo's handiwork. He made it in spring, when the willows are most pliant. You snap off a branch, cut a notch, tap the bark and twist it off. Then you deepen the notch and cut a plane about halfway through the notch end of the branch. You slip the bark back on and—there you are!—you have a willow whistle.

Phoooze-phooze. This is about the only sound I can play, like the bleating of a muntjac calf. When Momo tested the sound for me, it sounded like this: *waah waah–tcooot waah waah.* Grandpa can make the sound of a cloud of cicadas.

I raise the whistle up in the air and let Grandpa take a few puffs. No surprise: a rhythmic drone.

Leaving the thicket, I come to a wide open alpine space. Along the way grow cinnamon, laurel, and cherry trees, with cardamom and hibiscus shrubs. On a flowery blanket of pink and white throng bulbuls, like white-headed old men, drinking nectar. There are Japanese white-eyes too. It's a bustling scene, but I don't bother to look round at the splashes of colour. I need to scrutinize the path for clues. I am especially vigilant for footprints, hoping to find some sign of my one-time pet.

She is probably bigger now. I just hope she hasn't got too big.

Lately I've been finding bear droppings and prints on this path, but I don't know if they belong to my pet bear, the one I rescued and raised at home.

"She must be bigger now, but can her paws be that big?" I think to myself as I inspect several footprints on the ground.

As I look around, the sound of the birds calling and

insects crying starts to get on my nerves. I don't know whether I am hesitant or afraid. There is still a long way to go and I am stuck here, unsure of my next move.

I rescued Cub last summer. She was caught in a trap. I prised apart the metal jaws and carried her home. Father was sawing wood to make me a new stool. When he saw the cub I was holding in my arms, he stood up in shock.

"Momo, she's hurt!" I said.

Father tossed aside his saw and said, "How many times have I told you, kids aren't supposed to go climbing the mountain? It's too far from home and too dangerous." But as Father was telling me off, he couldn't help giving the cub a curious once over. He had said I wasn't supposed to climb the mountain, but not in a way that meant I was forbidden to go, just that I shouldn't go too far.

"Momo, can we keep her?"

Father checked the cub and looked me in the eye. "You're not to climb the mountain ever again."

"Ahhhh…" I didn't want to promise I wouldn't go.

"Don't you forget. Never again."

"Can we keep her?"

Momo looked disappointed and didn't say yes or no. He walked through the blue floral curtain that served as the door to the bedroom, returning promptly with the first aid kit. Sitting on the bench, he cleaned and disinfected the cub's wound. From where I was watching, the bear pelt was right behind him on the wall. Momo looked like a mother bear.

He attended to the wound every day, while I gathered provisions—stems, berries, minnows and crabs—to supplement the yams and radishes we had around the house.

Finally Cub got better. Father knew what I wanted, but he refused to let her stay. He said she would soon grow too big to be a pet.

Before we let her go, I drew countless portraits of her in my book of bears. The day we released her, she snuggled in my arms, sniffing and licking me, but when I set her on the ground she only made a few circles around me before dashing off.

Would she know my scent? Could she trail me, no matter where I went? There is a foreign proverb in the storybook Father bought me about a bear's keen sense of smell. When a needle falls in the forest, the bear smells it.

I believe it.

I've been coming up here a lot lately, following the route we took when we let Cub go. Once or twice she really has found me by my scent—only a couple of times, but each time was a pleasant surprise.

Yes, she would find me, but maybe only because I would bring a half-eaten can of fish.

My book says bears come whenever they smell fish. Obviously, this is an effective way to find bears. The danger is that big bears might come too.

I've never seen a real live adult bear. I don't know if I'd have the guts to meet one face to face. The reason I always bring a black umbrella and a water pistol with me is a recommendation in the book. The book says opening a black umbrella will scare bears away, and that you can squirt their eyes with chilli water if they come too close.

But the book only teaches how to avoid bears, not how to make friends with bears. Rather contradictorily, the book also says that bears have excellent hearing and will leave of their own accord if they hear people approaching.

Every time I see Cub, she has grown quite a bit. The moon mark on her chest has also been getting more and more conspicuous. The thing is, lately she's no longer been willing to eat yam or radish, only fish. I can't blame her for being a picky eater, as there are certainly lots of tasty things in the forest, particularly pine cones. Once up a tree, she can spend hours up there gorging herself on pine cones, tossing some down to me when she is too stuffed to eat them herself. Last time I pulled one apart and tasted the nut inside. It was really tasty. There is another, green fruit she often eats, but it is hot and bitter, like Father's betel nut. As for tender shoots, a bear favourite, there is an unlimited supply in the forest.

She can even find food by sniffing around for anthills on the ground or cocoons in the hollows of trees. Her speciality is finding bee pupae and honey. One time, she shook a hive from a tree into a stream and waded in after it. In no time, she fished out the hive, swam to the other shore and began feasting upon it. The poor bees either drowned or got squished between her powerful jaws. Another time she started shaking a tree, and out of a hollow came a swarm of bees! She closed her eyes, one paw protecting her mouth and nose, the other thrust into the hollow to rip out the hive inside. A swarm of bees couldn't faze her. Her fur was bee-proof armour. The only danger came later on when she started to enjoy this delicacy: bees besieged inside the hive might catch her by surprise and bite her on the nose.

When I got home I drew all these scenes in my book. When all the blank pages of the book were filled, I pasted in more and kept right on drawing.

But before the new pages were filled in, Cub just stopped appearing.

Maybe the book is right, that when bears grow big enough and their hearing gets keen enough, they'll leave as soon as people come near.

I crouch down, poring over the footprint. Could this be Cub's print? Could her paws possibly be this big?

I take out paper and pencil, put the paper on the ground and carefully trace the print.

3
Out of Sight

With nobody in the world to watch me, I continue my climb. It is bright and clear. I see forests of jade, terraced tea fields and groves of persimmon and peach trees; daylilies, camellias and azaleas carpet the slopes. When I finally reach the summit, I lean on a sturdy tree and catch my breath to the rhythm of the breeze. I forget my cares and feel as if I am a living branch of the tree, or as if I am a tree myself. I wave my arms: lofty clouds flood over the peak and layers of golden light come to rest on the treetop. Thrilled, I wave my arms again: scudding clouds and radiant light. I gaze around at the splendour, imagining myself godlike in power.

A god would have the thousand-mile eye. Unfortunately, I do not, though I can see pretty far, gazing down from on high at waterfalls, fogbound forests and hanging bridges.

The waterfalls pour down like unfurling strips of silk suspended from rock walls, forming staggered streams that meander down the slopes and over the plain. Shadows play over the hills, and through a clearing in the clouds I can see on the shore of a stream daylilies and bamboo shoots that people have set out to dry on the rocks. There are other signs of human activity. Smoke puffs from the chimneys of several houses; people must be making cane syrup inside. On a long bamboo frame jelly figs are drying in the sun. Further out, the old temple in the village looks as small as a star. The only school in the village is the size of a matchbox. I can see people walking around the temple and down the streets, but am not sure whether Father has set up his stand by the school, the village temple or in one of the markets.

Normally, Father sets up at the school gate. After class, kids come and pay a penny to play spin the wheel. The prize, pointed to by an arrow when the wheel stops, is one of Father's breadmen. Some kids keep spinning the wheel until they get the one they want.

Then there is Lotus.

Lotus is probably this very moment milling around with the others, touching the breadmen with her grimy hands or even licking them.

Once I heard Father tell her to stop it. The other kids don't like her dirtiness and won't accept a breadman if she has touched it. All Father could do that day was remove that breadman, give it to Lotus for free and tell her to get lost.

But that didn't solve the problem. Other kids started trying to use the same trick. They realized that with one lick they too could get a breadman without paying. Lots of kids were itching to try. Those who didn't want to be associated with Lotus in any way would pay, a little grudgingly—it only cost a penny, after all—and go off to enjoy their breadman in solitude.

Father would alternate between the school, the temple and the markets. But no matter where he went, Lotus would find him. When she wanted a breadman, she would sneak up and touch one. Father would yell at her and she would obediently huddle off to the side and watch the customers play spin the wheel, or gaze blankly up at the sky or off towards the hills.

All the local kids like Father's breadmen. Unfortunately Father is not always able to sell all of them. There are not that many kids in the village. Even if he took his wares around to all the nearby villages, there would still not be enough children.

When there is a temple fair, however, Father can make a killing. For last year's fair, Father made lots of "sacrificial" offerings out of dough for the village temple. The crowds gazed in wonder at the mock "fruits" piled high on the altar table. The entire mock table was a feast for the eyes. To me it was an amazing masterpiece of bread sculpture. There were twenty-four courses, twelve mountain fruits and twelve seafood delicacies, every one steaming and in vivid colour. Just looking at them made people's mouths water.

The temple fair is the busiest time of year in the village. Every family from miles around attends. Father always takes me to see the popular attractions like cloth puppet shows or martial arts demonstrations. There are also lots of food stands in the square in front of the temple selling tempting treats, like candied yams, Dragon's beard treats, pop-rice, corn on the cob and smoked boar meat. Even if all the shops in the village displayed all their food products at once, it would be nothing like the variety of the fair. What's more, after the ritual is over, they always distribute the offerings for free to the fair-goers. And I don't have to push and shove, because the temple reserves a share for Father and me.

But what I liked best last year was not the food but the martial arts performer, who was showing off his skills and hawking traditional tonics.

He was at one of the far corners of the square. People had gathered round him and started shouting.

I pushed through the crowd of onlookers. The tonic hawker had drawn a chalk circle and was splitting bricks and breaking chains with his bare hands inside. The crowd kept calling, "Do it again!"

But then he stopped performing and picked up what looked like a bottle of snake oil or a vial of snake oil pills. "Please, folks, a moment of your time. You see these rippling muscles, like I have tendons of bronze and bones of iron? It's all thanks to this special preparation that I call Ursine Bile Miracle Medication. It's the most wonderful wonder drug in the whole wide world. It's made from a secret recipe that's been in my family for I don't know how many generations. We take eight times eight kinds of herbs and roots—sorry, I can't tell you which ones— extract the essences, and mix them with bile from a real live bear. It's a guaranteed cure-all, effective against bumps and bruises, swellings and sores, carbuncles and cancers. It also has amazing benefits for those who are well—just look at me! And if you don't believe me, step right up and try it for yourselves."

But the villagers didn't fork out their money. Someone yelled, "Less spiel and more substance! You think we're impressed by those old tricks and that load of tortoiseshit? Show us the real kung fu!"

The others joined in, "Yeah, show us what you're made of!"

Seeming more and more like a huckster, he moved right to the centre of the circle: "Folks, this is your lucky day. I don't show this one to just anyone, but today I'll make an exception." He dragged out a bed of nails and, excruciatingly slowly, lay down on it.

A hush fell over the crowd. Several people gasped.

I don't remember whether he was bleeding when he stood up, because for the whole performance I hid my head, looking only at his bear, which he kept off in a corner in a cage with a black cover.

Aside from that bear cub I'd rescued, I'd never been so close to a bear in my whole life. Off in the shadows, he seemed very calm, but maybe there was a lurking danger there. The performer didn't let people go near the bear, so I waited until he was busy with his nails to sneak over beside the cage. The black cover did not quite reach the base of the cage. When I looked in, I saw a tuft of black fur, nothing more.

Suddenly I was blinded by one of those cheap old electric spotlights.

The tonic hawker growled at me, "Kid, get away from the cage! Don't crouch there! He's a mean one. If you're not careful, he'll bite you!"

Everyone's eyes settled upon the cage.

"Dear friends, I told you my prescription contains authentic bear bile? Well, right here's a real live bear."

Everyone started to hoot and holler.

"How are we supposed to see it when it's covered up like that?"

"Remove the cloth, remove the cloth!"

The performer told everyone to be quiet so as not to excite the bear. "You people simply do not know what a ferocious bear this is! Usually I keep him covered, so he'll think it's night and go into deep, deep hibernation. But once light shines in his eyes, he'll be roused to life again. He might start howling. He might even break out of his cage! If he does, it'll be too late."

Then someone shouted, "But if you keep him under wraps like this, what are we supposed to look at?"

"A spectacle nobody else in the world has ever seen…" The performer edged over to the cage and lifted up the cover partway. By the light of that old spotlight in the centre of the square, we all caught a glimpse of a furry form inside.

"Look, everybody, look!"

The performer put a big piece of paper and a pencil by the cage and cracked his leather whip. Slowly, the bear extended half a furry arm through the bars of the cage, picked up the pencil and wrote a single word: *URSINE*. I tugged on an adult's sleeve. "Ursine," the person said, "it means bear." Now ursine is not a word everyone knows or is even able to spell. It took the bear a few tries to get it right. And when he did, everyone started clapping and asking him to write another word. The performer cracked his whip again, and the bear started writing out another word: *BILE*. The crowd clicked their tongues in admiration. Another crack of the whip. A hush. Another word and sighs of amazement! All the dogs in the area started barking, excited by all the commotion.

A cold, dreary wind was blowing. The bear started calling. It sounded anxious and sorrowful, like it was whining, but the whines became growls, and the growls became howls. The salesman gave a few more cracks of his whip.

"It's too bright. His eyes are used to the dark. If he's exposed to the light for too long, he'll go berserk!"

The salesman walked round the cage and pulled down the cover as far as it would go. The howls immediately stopped.

He lifted up the paper so all the onlookers could see the words, written in a crooked scrawl: *URSINE BILE MIRACLE MEDICINE.*

The square was buzzing with argument. "A writing bear!"

"Are you sure it's a bear?"

"I say it is."

"But you can't deny that the guy was careful to keep the inside of the cage out of sight, so we don't know if it's really a bear or not."

"Even if it's not a bear, it's pretty amazing for an animal to be able to write, eh?"

"Okay, okay, okay, now look here." The performer started to walk around the circle. "Your humble servant here has a question for those of you who bought a package of my special pills last time. Did they do the trick? Were they effective? If there's anyone here who used this miracle medication without any healthful effect, let him speak up."

Silence.

The performer made another round. "Some say we itinerant tonic hawkers are dishonest, that all we know how to do is bluster and blow our own horns. Well, folks, I'm here to tell you I neither blow nor crow. And take my word for it: you buy these here pills, you'll suffer no ills…" Then he took a look around and chose a person in the audience. "Please, reverend sir, would you consent to come up for a second? No no, no charge, no charge whatsoever."

This elderly man was half-pulled into the circle. The performer cordially greeted him and asked about his health.

Then the performer addressed the audience: "I have never seen this gentleman before in my life. If anyone can prove the contrary, he's welcome to speak now." He looked around again. Nobody spoke. "Now, he says his shoulder blade and tailbone are bothering him. I guarantee that with my Ursine Bile Miracle Medication I can make him better in no time at all."

Everyone watched as the old man took two pills and the performer started massaging and manipulating his tired old bones. When the old man stood up again, his body had limbered up a fair bit. He cheerfully returned to his place in the audience, and there was another burst of heated discussion. The performer asked for another volunteer: "Who else wants to give it a try?" Lots of people pressed forward. He again chose someone elderly, asked the nature of the person's illness, and shortly had his patient on the road to recovery.

Everyone began pushing for a place at the front, so the performer rushed around handing out numbers, saying, "Please, no shoving, there's no hurry, please wait your turn. Take a look at the number on the card. Everyone will get a free consultation, don't you worry."

People in the crowd waiting to see the quack doctor watched with fascination as he diagnosed and prescribed, as if they were witnessing a miracle, especially foolish Lotus, who was crouching wide-eyed off to the side. Didn't she know that people could see her panties when she crouched down like that?

Though Lotus is about fifteen years old, she is still in a class with nine year olds. I heard she spent three years in the first class, and I don't know how many times she repeated the next school year. Nobody's ever given her special attention. I feel sorry for Lotus. Her family don't love her. They never give her an allowance for fear she'll be cheated out of it. That's not to say she is necessarily cheated much at school. She is like an old joke you've heard too many times. Even crybabies and wimps don't bother to try to bully her, because she doesn't seem to realize she is being bullied. She never reacts, so bullies find her boring and quickly lose interest.

I never bully her, either. I just find her troublesome. Or even annoying, because Lotus seems to like me. She is always appearing by my side to see what I am doing, and more often than not she gets in my way. Like on the day of the fair, I wanted to sneak over again to see the bear while there was such a crowd in the square, but Lotus was blocking the way. Then I had an idea: I pulled Lotus over to the cage with me, so I could hide behind her bulk. I took out my picture book, laid a pencil on top of it and put it before the bear, as a request for it to honour me with a word or two. For ages the bear didn't move. I pushed the book even nearer and made sure he could see my "offering", a fairy peach made of flour. Eventually, it extended its paw towards the peach. I pointed towards the book and pencil. Finally, the bear gripped the pencil and made a few marks on the page to see if that would be enough for me.

Graced by the signature of a real bear, my book now seemed glossier somehow. And every picture of a bear inside was now somehow more personalized and unique, as if it had been autographed.

I went to find Father, who was drinking in front of the temple, and waited until the banquet was over. Then we returned home.

What an exciting evening it had been! I forget when I fell asleep or what happened to that fairy peach. Did the bear take it? Did I drop it before it could get it into the cage? I asked Father, but he had been too drunk to remember anything, even how we got home.

The next day, I drew an invisible bear in a cage with a black cover. All you could see of him was half a paw clutching a peach.

But even from that half a paw, you could tell the bear was probably thin. The medicine salesman had said his pills had bear bile in them, and this bear was probably his living bile supply.

But did he really pierce the bear's gallbladder, to tap it for bile? Wouldn't that be painful? I can't wait until this year's temple fair, when like the grownups I'll ask the tonic hawker to lift the cover all the way and let me have a better look.

I go up to an even higher ridge and gaze down. Father has probably set up by the road. But I still can't see him.

Suddenly I hear a piercing cry.

I look up to find where it came from: a white-eyed thrush flies overhead from right to left.

I start running after it.

4
A Manifest Mystery

Oazmu—nowadays people call it white-eyed thrush—is the reincarnation of a great warrior of our people. We augur by the oazmu. For hunting parties, a magnificent call of an oazmu is auspicious, but a sorrowful call is inauspicious; an oazmu that flies left to right is a bad sign, but one that flies from right to left is a good sign...

I head west, down the mountain.

On the way down, my whole body feels light, carried along on currents of air, with superlative grace. And the cool breezes, butterfly shadows, bird calls and insect cries make me feel wide open and carefree. But further down the sun appears from behind the clouds and its rays start burning my head. To keep from fainting, I duck into a grove of jelly fig trees.

It is refreshing and cool inside, but the turquoise of the trees, the smell of rot and mould and the light milky mist give me a bad feeling. I feel like a formless force is leading me by the arm. I want to resist but I can't.

Underfoot there are moss, fallen leaves and hister beetles crawling all over the ground. There is also a pulsating buzzing or humming sound. In the dim light, I can still make out some green grasshoppers darting here and there. I drag my foot over the ground to brush aside the thick layer of moss and leaves. Underneath this layer is the trace of a trail.

Has someone been here lately?

Maybe there is someone here now, but I haven't seen anyone on the way.

Inside the grove are several pieces of coral. Washed colourless by corroding time, these pitted hunks are thickly covered by a layer of decaying leaves, through which ants, hoppers, centipedes and spiders crawl. I walk past the coral and brush aside snakelike threads of beard lichen blocking the way. A ray of sunlight penetrates the canopy and shines on a big beautiful conch shell, like a burst of silver in a crypt. It's as if someone has brushed aside a camouflage of lichen and leaves to reveal a mystery to me.

Gingerly, I dig out the shell. The texture of the surface is rough, and there are round holes the size of needles that form a weird pattern, like a secret sign. I press my lips close and blow. The sound is remote, like a syllable in an ancient spell that I heard in a dream and have followed here.

Outside the grove, the path continues to the left. I soon

come to a cliff.

Here, its roots gnarled right into the rock, grows a giant cypress tree. This is actually a platform jutting out halfway up a cliff, the way a shoulder juts out from a neck. Down below is Devil's Gulch. I have to be careful, lest I fall into the canyon, which is tortuous, fathomless and dark. There are always weird sounds coming from it: one time I was startled by the thunderous sound of beating wings as thousands of bats gushed out of the chasm and flooded the sky.

Even though Devil's Gulch is scary, I come here to the shoulder of the cliff every couple of days, because of an elfinwood called the Enchanted Thicket. The cypress is one of the trees in the Enchanted Thicket.

I named it myself. There are lots of bizarrely shaped trees, some with large lumps covering their roots, some extending claw-like branches, some with roots like octopus tentacles and even some like centipedes, spiders and crabs.

Among them is a tree like a bat with wings outspread. This particular tree contains a secret of mine and Cub's. Whenever I come, I always put something to eat in a box which I have placed in the hollow in the bat tree: sweets, cakes or breadmen Father hasn't been able to sell. On the box I have carved the likeness of a bear.

The opening to the hollow wasn't originally so big, but one time Cub widened it considerably with her claws while yanking out a beehive. Putting the wooden box in there was an idea I had later—I was sure Cub would smell the treats inside when she came near.

I get out the box and open it, discovering the treats I left last time are untouched. In the past few months, the stuff in the box has often gone stale or rotten or been nibbled by ants. I am disappointed every time, of course, but I keep cleaning it out and leaving fresh treats inside.

Once today's treats are safely stored, I put the box back and lean on a gravestone by the tree, speaking silently to Grandpa, who lies beneath.

Whether it is really my grandfather I don't know, but I feel he is there. When I pray for things, he appears and presents me with what I've asked for. Like last year I wished for a bear cub, and he arranged for that trap to be set, for Cub to step in it, and for me to find her…

Grandpa was sent up the mountains late in the Japanese occupation, in the 1930s or 1940s, to be a camphorman. At the time, camphor wood was an important commodity, so the Japanese ordered the Taiwanese people, especially the aborigines, to log it. Grandpa didn't want to go to the Philippines to serve as a military porter in the war against the Americans, and working as a camphor logger was the only other option.

My grandmother was the daughter of a shaman. Too bad I never saw her. I heard that before she died she said she wanted to climb the mountain to where the moon shone brightest and meet her husband, my grandfather, who had become the Guardian of the Celestial Spirit. According to shamanic lore, the Celestial Spirit is a glowing giant clothed in bearskin, while its Guardian is a giant bear. Grandmother's ashes were scattered at the brightest spot on the mountain—right here in the Enchanted Thicket—

as she instructed. But nobody is sure if Grandpa is really buried here, only that a lot of camphormen were killed near here during a B29 air raid. The villagers dug a pit and threw all the charred remains into it. There was nothing they could do for those who had died deeper or higher in the mountains. But even so I am sure that Grandpa can really hear me praying to him. Cub's appearance in my life was proof of that. Even if I only got to keep Cub for a short time, I still believe Grandpa is here.

"Grandpa! Grandpa!" I murmur. "I've brought you another shell. Look how big it is! What spirit does it represent?"

I turn the shell over and put my ear close to the gravestone.

"Evil Dispeller?"

What? Evil Dispeller? No… It's Hunting Companion.

I quickly dig into the ground beside the gravestone, find the urn buried there, open it up and put the shell inside. Then I return the urn to the ground.

"It's hidden now, Grandpa."

Even when he doesn't say anything, I can feel his response.

Maybe Grandpa is everywhere, sometimes just a beam of light, a gust of wind, at other times a moonshadow or a leaf. Sometimes he lies inside the grave sleeping soundly —I need to call several times to wake him. Sometimes he appears unannounced before me.

Lately his voice has been muffled, probably because his beard has grown too long. I pick up a rock and scrape the moss off the gravestone. Now Grandpa's face is clean.

No words are etched on the stone, but it is by no means unmarked. I always draw something on it by scraping with a stone or by dipping my finger into the mud. When my drawings get washed off I just draw them on again. I always draw the same thing: scenes from the story of a bear, which is Grandpa's story.

I am sure it's Grandpa's story. It is a mystery into which I have been initiated and which I draw to make it real. When I bury a shell or draw the pictures on the gravestone, the melody of a ritual song sung by a chorus of many warriors starts coming from the centre of the grove. The words sound like this:

> *i likihli likihli iui i lavahli lavahli*
> *ina muli vengeeli iui mulilalee vuai*
> *ina mataru taruuhl iui matalalee vuai*
> *ina hlisapeta vinau i saramarukaruka*
> *ina vengavenga vihluua i kupatarahlapee*
> *kupatarahlapee kumiakui iaiai*

Somehow, though I don't speak this language, I understand what the words mean:

> *The spleenwort fronds in moonlight clear the fog,*
> *And flames are dancing on a ribwood log.*
> *Our patewood cups are filled with mead and grog,*
> *Beneath the routbaum roasts a feral hog.*

And then I hear Grandpa chanting.

*Our tribe has in total twelve Sacred Shells, one for each
Tribal Spirit:*

Guardian Protector, grant us many offspring;
Hunting Companion, grant us abundant game;
Peace Patron, grant us safety and well-being;
Inspiration Whisperer, grant us skill and fame;

Valorous Warrior, grant us fearlessness in the fight;
Evil Dispeller, grant us deliverance;
Victory Guarantor, grant us vigour and might;
Work Leader, grant us diligence;

Weather Master, grant us favourable wind and rain;
Weariness Chaser, keep us in good form;
Sustenance Bringer, grant us full stores of grain;
Health Preserver, keep us safe and warm…

A mystery has been made manifest. I have undergone a
rite of passage.

5

Irrepressible Happiness

By the time I leave the Enchanted Thicket, it is already almost noon. The woods are hot and humid now. Lucky I have a resting place, a secluded ravine on the other side of the mountain, with a pool and a waterfall. The waterfall is tiered—when the water reaches the final tier, it glides over an overhang into a plunge pool below. The pool is cool and clear, with schools of fish and shrimp and with moss and grasses growing on its damp shore. There are several hoary pines and firs hanging with beard lichen, like trolls draped in silken streamers. I can't wait to strip off my sweaty clothes. I choose a place to go in, a slab of moss-covered rock. Once in the water, I submerge myself completely, letting the cool water penetrate my skin and dispel the summer heat from every pore. There is a deep end and a shallow end. I swim a few laps until I am tired, then sit in the shallows. Fish swim around me, but I don't have the strength to shoo them away. In fact, I just lean back and let them dart among my limbs. A little ticklish, but overall it is pleasant. Sometimes, though, I have to flick away little frogs who like to lick me with their sticky tongues, which tickles and leaves me itchy. For a time, I just sit, thinking of nothing, whiling away the minutes. It is so nice and cool, and there are brilliantly coloured mountain flowers and butterflies fluttering, like I've been transported to a fairyland.

But I cannot afford to let my guard down. That old song has reminded me of some of Grandpa's warnings: Near a grove of ribwood trees, be wary of the water. If you see a patewood tree it means you'll have strange luck today. And if you see a routbaum tree, be on the lookout for enemies. There are some ribwoods on the slope by the stream behind the cabin. I've seen a patewood tree in a dream —but I don't know what this warning means, because my luck is pretty strange every day. Those small, normal-looking trees by the pool—those are routbaum. Although I've heeded another of Grandpa's warnings and plucked spleenwort along the way as a talisman, I know I have to be vigilant in case I meet my enemies. Unfortunately, I don't know where they are.

I stand up in the water and realize my stomach is growling; so I go into the woods to cut several lengths of bamboo and pull up bamboo shoots. I put the shoots with rice and salt into the tubes. Then I bury them in the ground and start a fire on top. Soon I will have my lunch.

Perhaps not soon enough, though, as it takes a long time to cook this way. While I am waiting, I tiptoe into a tussock of grass to look for yokebugs, greyish-green insects that are hard to find. I saw someone probe with his foot like this and catch a yokebug in no time flat. The yokebug as a rule is fat and round. If you catch one by the legs it'll start kowtowing to you. It's quite amusing. I soon catch enough yokebugs for a side dish, and spear them with a long blade of grass. First we play locomotive, then tug of war. The mock battles soon get repetitious, and leave the bugs gasping for breath—even if I set them free they probably won't last long. That's what I tell myself, but actually I am mostly thinking of my hungry belly. I spit the yokebugs over the fire—the oily kebab is soon crackling away, giving off a mouthwatering smell. They'll make a crispy snack.

Unfortunately, I soon gobble them up but the rice still isn't ready. Though even a dozen yokebug kebabs don't make a meal, I am getting addicted to them. I decide to look for more.

There are lots of bugs on the ground, but not all of them are fit for human consumption. I have to find the plumpest, tenderest and juiciest. While checking every tree and tuft of grass nearby, I find a small hole. I start digging, knowing I've found a stash of rare delicacies. Inside are the whitish larvae of cicadas that must have been practising the mystic arts of the underground for six or seven years now. Out here in the wilderness, I have no oil to fry them with, but even cooked over an open fire they are delicious.

But roasting and eating the cicadas doesn't take long, either. The minutes are crawling by. I don't want to sit waiting for the rice to cook, so I clamber onto a boulder, above me a waterfall, beside me leafy shade. I sit like the eminent monks I've seen in kung fu movies, but I have no idea what kind of special power I can acquire just sitting here like this.

The sun slowly lowers past the tips of the trees, and around one of the higher waterfalls a faint rainbow appears. Am I sitting at one end of the arc? My ears are filled with the reverberating sound of water falling, it seems, everywhere: it must be falling onto stone terraces and into pools. It gives me the feeling of mystery, like the harmony of an ancient song you've only ever heard in a dream.

I'm enjoying the cool, refreshing breeze, which blows through the leaves and the hollows of the trees. Water and wind are like two sections in a mighty, swelling orchestra. Before I know it I've closed my eyes and drifted into a deep realm of vastness, feeling as if my body has evaporated, leaving my mind to roam free.

The sun is now even lower in the sky. The sunshine slants through the breaks in the leaves and sprinkles onto my body. I awake with a start, afraid that my lunch has been burnt to a crisp. I blow out the flames, get out the bamboo tubes and split them open. The rice is cooked to perfection.

A mission of monkeys has arrived on the trail of the scent. Birds take notice.

I let some bits of rice fall to the ground. Several bolder birds come down to peck them up before returning to their perches.

At first the monkeys sit and watch—any young ones

that start to approach are immediately clutched back by their mothers.

In the mission there is a big male watching me. He edges forward step by step, until finally he is crouching right in front of me.

I know this means he's planning to attack.

He glares at me. I look away, ignoring him. But then he jumps up and stands face to face.

He wants to stare me down.

I look to the side, indicating that I will not fight. He keeps his eyes fixed upon me.

I simply close my eyes.

When I take a look, he is still there. I bare my teeth to scare him. He does the same, but then, looking down, he slowly retreats. I know he's taken fright.

The male returns to the mission with nothing to show for his efforts.

A female waits until I am not looking and tosses a branch that knocks one of the bamboo tubes right out of my hand. Before I have time to react, she's stolen the tube and taken it to share with her young.

What a clever trick! The little monkeys press round her and in no time have gobbled up all the rice. Shamed, the male monkeys return to the trees.

A young monkey starts to imitate his mother by finding food. He extends his paw towards a brocaded snake hanging on a rock wall. But his mother intervenes like an arrow and yanks him away by the scruff of the neck. The snake stays frozen for a moment, then slithers down the wall and into the bushes.

The monkeys climb to the tops of the tallest trees, where they get busy grooming one another and play-fighting. One young male suddenly waltzes up to the alpha male and waves his tail. It seems to be a challenge, but it just takes a few slaps to force him to beat a retreat. Safe on his throne, the alpha enjoys the attentions of the females. Several older females handle his upper body, while a young female crouches by his tail. After inspecting his powerful loins, she grasps and lifts the tail in one hand and combs through the fine hair between his buttocks with the other. When she finds lice she pops them into her mouth, chewing noisily and licking her lips in satisfaction. Later on she simply buries her head in the crack of the male's backside.

The sun is setting behind the top of the valley. The light, now quite low, pulls a large and brilliant rainbow from the lowest waterfall. There really are seven hues, I enthuse, as I count the bands of colour. It is so vivid, a celestial miracle.

Each time I come here, I wait for the rainbow to reach down to me and cup its arc into my hands. Then I like to skirt the pond to the edge of the last fall, squeeze through the opening between the screen of water and the rock. Behind the screen is another world, a rock shelter, which opens up into Cataract Cave. It is my own discovery, the one I am proudest of. Looking out, you see spray tinted by sunlight. It is divine, a kind of vaporized magic potion that is known to me alone. I catch droplets of it on my tongue and feel myself transforming once again into a being of air.

There are three areas in the cave. The front, closest to the screen of water, is a broad bed of rock, in which there are sinks of different sizes. Spring water drips down from the ceiling, forming pools in the sinks. Higher up, away from the sinks, is a platform with a dry depression, shaped almost like a baby's cradle. There is space enough inside for one: lying in the cradle looking up, you see glowworms at the ceiling of the cave like a constellation of stars. There are strange veins and indentations in the walls, which put into relief the forms of flying dragons, floating clouds, shooting stars and crescent moons. The deeper indentations are actually big enough to store things in—I call them Treasure Troves, and from time to time leave toys, rations and nuts in them. I've drawn a treasure map and keep a regular inventory.

There is already enough treasure in the cave for a bear to winter here. I wish Cub would enjoy what I've left for her. Although I've found claw marks on the trunks of trees near the cave and prints by the pool, Cub has never touched the things in the Treasure Troves.

Cub knows about this cave, though. Last summer, I brought her to the pool to learn how to swim and catch fish. We went into the cave when we got tired and lay down in the stone cradle for a snooze. Cub was already getting so big I couldn't hold her any more. She would often squeeze me out. Later on there was only space for Cub… but why had she stopped coming to this cradle, which now was all hers? I put strips of cloth inside as a mattress, but lately I haven't seen the impression of her body. Maybe Cub has got too big to fit inside the cradle.

The middle area of the cave is a labyrinth of intersecting tunnels, some so narrow you have to go sideways or even crawl to get through. But as you pass out of the labyrinth to the back—the innermost area—there is a wonder to behold: a chamber with translucent stalactites growing from the ceiling. There is another way out from this chamber—so that the cave is actually a tunnel—but the opening is small, high, and mostly blocked off by a swallow's nest. You can hear baby swallows cheeping inside the nest. Once I moved a rock over and, standing on tiptoe, plucked the nest down and hid it in one of the Treasure Troves, planning to wait for the eggs to hatch. Too bad that when I wasn't looking, Cub went and crushed all the eggs. Later she put several similar sized rocks in the nest, like she was making up for a crime, but covering up too.

It gets dark early in the cave. As soon as the sunlight starts dimming, it seems like night inside. I have to get a move on while there is still light, because at nightfall Father will return home.

Also before dark, something else will come out: when the streetlamps at the edge of the village come on, the demon heads will gather.

I call them demon heads. Others in the village call them snakehead moths or bat moths. The pattern on the wings of these monsters is uncannily like the shape of a pair of fiendish horns. When a swarm of them flies towards your face, it is as scary as a cloud of bats against the sky at Devil's Gulch. There are more demon head moths in these parts than you might expect. Most of them are raised by Lotus's family.

Her father originally tended a guava orchard. When he saw demon head caterpillars on his fruit, he flicked them away and stomped on them. Later he changed his mind. He collected a whole bunch of moths, putting them to pasture in a guava orchard, saying he wanted to preserve and export them. It sounded like a crazy get-rich-quick scheme. Every guava was soon nibbled rotten. Lotus's father was all smiles. He claimed these were the "world's biggest" moths, each one worth two hundred guavas. His orchard soon became the biggest moth nursery in the village. He saw each one as a crisp and shiny banknote and weighed each cocoon by fractions of a gram. I've seen workmen in the moth barn use wire and cardboard to suspend the pregnant queen moths in midair, with only their smooth bellies exposed to make egg collection easier. It seemed like some sick kind of torture. The orchard is now enclosed by fine netting, to protect the caterpillars from the birds. Through the layers of bird netting, you can see thousands of gruesome caterpillars climbing all around the orchard. It is enough to make you want to gag.

I blinker my eyes and hurry round the village, not daring to give them a single glance. The moths fluttering around the streetlamp might be escapees, or maybe they are simply wild. In any case, they are terrifying.

What's more, they might be cursed.

Lotus said a bird went blind after running into a streetlamp. When she picked it up, there were demon heads sucking on its eyes. Lotus pulled the moths away, and where the eyes had been two black holes were gaping, like the eye sockets of a skull.

6
Will-o'-the-wisp

Father always brings something home to eat, fire-roasted boar meat, peas stir-fried with jelly figs, tiger lily soup or star anise chicken wings. Tonight the house light is burnt out. I sit in the dark eating and waiting for Father to find the candles. Once Father lights a candle and places it on the table, I sense a pair of eyes outside the window staring at me, which reminds me of the gaping eye holes of that poor bird whose eyes were eaten by the demon heads. It is a really weird feeling. It gives me such a fright that I lower my head, not daring to look towards the window or even think about who or what might be outside.

After dinner, Father gets out his ingredients and prepares tomorrow's wares. I crouch off to the side, watching him work. He deftly mixes glutinous rice flour and wheat flour, adds water, adjusts the moisture, kneads the dough, sections it, boils it, kneads it a second time, adds sugar and banana oil and then forms the pieces into different figures. Next he mixes the candy colours and begins applying them. He usually demonstrates something and gives me a few pieces to practise on.

"Peach plus neutral gives flesh colour. Orange plus black gives walnut. Blue plus yellow and neutral gives grass green…" Occasionally he will look up and ask, "Understand?"

"Understand," I say, though I see that the colours I've mixed are not quite the same as Father's. This is a problem of proportion. But I don't really care whether my colours are standard or not. I am just having fun.

Today the breadmen sold out, but now Father is making one especially for me. First he pinches out an oval shape and colours it red, asking me to guess which character he is preparing to make.

"Lord Guan."

"Right!" Pleased, Father nods, then starts to work on the face. He asks me if I remember the story of the origin of breadmen.

I say I remember.

I can see from the expression on his face that he sees through my fib. "You say you remember, but last time I told you, you fell asleep before I finished." He gets me to bring my stool over, and tells me the story again as we sit knee to knee.

"Long ago, during the Era of the Three Kingdoms, Zhuge

Liang attacked a people called the Southern Savages. Seven times he captured King Meng Huo, the fierce chieftain of the savages, and seven times he let him go…"

Here Father stops to ask, "Did I make it this far last time?" I nod, not daring to look him in the eye. Father keeps making Lord Guan's face, not looking to see whether I really want to hear the rest of the story. "Zhuge Liang won the campaign, but on the way home he reached a river called the River Lu. His army was ready to ford the river, when suddenly a great wind arose and nearly capsized the boats. Zhuge Liang called Meng Huo and asked him what was going on. Meng Huo replied that the warriors buried by the river were making waves because they couldn't go home to reunite with their families. If Zhuge Liang wanted to make it across, he had to sacrifice seven times seven —forty-nine—human heads to the lonely ghosts of these warriors. Zhuge Liang said that in war death is inevitable; but if he killed forty-nine innocent soldiers now, their spirits would wander lonely too, and there would never be peace upon the earth. Zhuge Liang mulled it over, and then told his cook to use rice flour to make forty-nine head-shaped skins, and then stuff them with horsemeat and beef. They threw the effigies into the river and crossed without incident."

Several mosquitoes are buzzing round my head. I wait for them to stop in the shadows on the side of my leg and then grab them. This is my speciality: catching mosquitoes live is so much more fun than killing them. I turn them over, holding them lightly between two fingers, then pluck out their stingers and relax my hand. This may sound strange, but stinger-less mosquitoes cannot fly. Legs quivering, they can only sort of crawl around. They have no expression, but seem full of hatred, as if you have castrated them. Step by step, they come at you, beating their wings a couple of times, but they can't fly any more.

Maybe they are filled with hatred, or maybe they are just in terrible pain. I pretend not to see, continuing to focus on the breadman in Father's hand. But I still feel wary.

I sit, unmoving now, eyeing the window. My hair is practically standing on end.

I feel something moving underfoot. A little gecko hops out of the shadow of the table and then back in. I don't let Father see. I put out my hand to grip it round the belly, turn away, take the Monkey brand matchbook out of my pocket and put the gecko inside. The gecko is so small and dopey-looking it's cute. I have a pet to take care of for a few minutes. I give him a couple of mosquitoes to eat and let him go. When you treat a gecko this way, it might not feel any gratitude towards you, but at least you haven't scared it to death, and at least it won't pretend you don't exist.

Father has finished the face and is now using other tools —scissors, a comb, a horntip and a toothpick—to make the helmet, the arms and legs, the boots and shirt and the battle gown. Last but not least is Lord Guan's famous sword, with a crescent moon-shaped blade and a dragon design on the hilt. A spirited Lord Guan appears before my eyes.

Father lets me hold the breadman and then hurries me off to bed.

I drag my feet. Instead of lying in bed, I lift the floral

curtain around the bed and spy on Father as he makes his breadmen. Father orders me to lie down.

To be honest, tonight's present is a disappointment. This Lord Guan isn't as likable as the Sun Wukong he made last time. Probably it isn't as tasty as Sun Wukong, either. Father thinks I don't like Sun Wukong, the Monkey King from Journey to the West, because whenever he gives me a Monkey King, I just carry it around or put it down somewhere in my room until it goes stale instead of eating it. A Monkey King breadman doesn't keep long—just a day or two. Father said he'd make me some with salt and alum that would last a long time. But they'd be inedible. I said I didn't want ones like that. I wanted him to keep making the sweet ones. And I still wanted a Monkey King. The truth is that I couldn't bear to eat a Monkey King. That is true for other figures as well, but those I leave in the hollow of the tree for Cub, even though they quickly go stale there too.

This Lord Guan doesn't strike my fancy, at least not for the time being. I put him on the windowsill, hoping the fresh air will extend his life. At the same time he can scare whatever is "out there". I feel there is a pair of eyes outside the window, that ever since Father started making breadmen, the house has been under surveillance. But I don't dare open the window all the way to prove it, and I don't want to tell Father. Maybe Cub has come back. Or maybe not.

I wake up in the middle of the night. I don't know when Father came to bed. I must have been sound asleep by then. Every so often I am aware of those eyes outside the window and of bumping and flapping sounds from inside the room, from the beams overhead. I know there is nothing to be afraid of from inside the room, though, because these sounds from the rafters are made by bats roosting in our house. They don't make any trouble for us and even do us some good, by brushing away mosquitoes from our faces when we are sleeping. They always vanish before dawn.

The eyes outside are another matter entirely. Eventually, I can't stand it any more, get on my nightgown and squeeze through the crack at the bottom of the window. Around the cabin are the spooky shadows of trees. The stars twinkle through the clouds. Spring water trickles down the slope. Those thirsty butterflies must have gone to roost with the birds. The moon shines on the water, making the black mountain slope appear to bleed silver blood. There are several clumps of reeds off in the marsh, out of which glowing lights float—the glowworms skim the water and fly into the marsh, flickering as they go. The glowworms and the stars look at each other in the watery mirror of the marsh. The breeze ripples the water and turns the points of light into silvery tracks. Now you cannot tell which tracks are of glowworms and which are of stars.

In the clumps of reeds, I see clusters of eggs shining with a pale light. After giving birth all together, their mothers die, leaving the eggs to hatch into larvae on their own. The larvae shine with a greenish-blue light. At nightfall someday soon they will come crawling out; during daylight hours, they will hide in the mud. When spring approaches, their bodies will mature; then they will dig a hole in the mud and pupate. They will lie low for a season until the weather gets hot, maturing inside their light yellow cocoons and finally bursting out in summer as terrestrial shooting stars. Every year it's the same.

I feel a presence; an impossibly old man is beside me. He takes me by the hand. He is the one who teaches me the secrets of the night. The moon shines on the forest, the stream on the slope and the reeds in the marsh. It casts a silver glow on the window.

As we stand there, we hear out of the sky the strains of a song. It is a hunting song called The Ballad of Hlalumalumai:

nasicui rumahlaree rumaihlaveesa
ihlaveesa imiravusa vulahla
vulahla ui hlalumalumai
Hlalumalumai hlimahlulailai ampulai laita iaiaai

Our Hlalumalumai went missing while chasing a boar.
It's three years already—Where went she? What for?
O who now is barking, way down in the South?
It's Hlalumalumai and puppies with boars in the mouth.

And I hear Grandpa say, *This song is one we sing at spirit rituals. It tells the story of a hunter who adopted a dog, faithful and true, named Hlalumalumai. One day they went deep into the mountains to hunt. Hlalumalumai ran off in pursuit of a boar. The hunter looked everywhere but could find neither hide nor hair of Hlalumalumai. He kept searching until it started to rain. He had to give up. Three years later, Hlalumalumai with twelve canine sons in tow reappeared at the hunter's side while he was on a trek south. Each son carried a boar in its jaws.*

Grandpa joins in the singing, and the chorus keeps repeating, over and over again, softer and softer, lulling me off to…

7
Concerning the Soul

Morning again! It's still quite early, but Father is already outside. I prop myself on the windowsill and watch him shoulder his load and drag his feet away, swaying. That load isn't light, though it isn't that heavy either, probably the same weight as me when I was younger. When I was little, Father would hoist a two-sided basket: in one side was his stuff and in the other side was me. Later I started getting too big for him to carry around. Without me, the load must be easier to manage. Still, he seems to be having difficulty. I think once I grow up I will take the load and put it in a big basket on one side, with a comfy seat for Father on the other side. Where will I take him? That's a tough question.

Once I asked Father where he wants to go. He simply said, "Where your mother went." Grandpa had told me my mother was resting on the mountain and that if I wanted to find her resting place I would need the moon to guide me. I originally planned to kill a bug at night and follow its spirit to see where the moon would take it. But then it occurred to me that I am scared of the dark. Killing a bug at night would be no problem. The problem would be going outside when it's dark. I wouldn't dare, except maybe in a dream. I'm scared of the unknown watcher outside the window and those demon head moths as well —they might eat human eyes too! And what if the moon only guides the souls of people of my tribe? Would the moon help lowly insects find the way home? Where do bugs go after they die? This last problem really bothers me, but Grandpa hasn't told me.

Maybe they have their own place to go, or maybe they don't go anywhere. If so, there are a lot of praying mantis spirits in the house, as lately Father has been feeding me two heaped spoonfuls of roasted mantis powder before bed every night. I asked him not to kill any more mantises. He said if I stop having nightmares he will stop feeding me them. I have no idea why I cry like this in the middle of the night. Momo says I sound like a wolf howling at the moon. I suspect I might be humming the tune of a ritual song.

Outside the window a praying mantis comes to rest on a branch. It's a female. She sways on the thin branch, and in no time a male joins her, with another male close by. The other one hurries over, but it is not fast enough, as the female has already decided to go with the first one, which is riding on her body, their two tails curled tightly together. The other male seems to have missed the boat, but after circling them a few times, he just gets up on the back of the male, like he can't tell boy and girl apart. Maybe he thinks this is better than nothing. Or maybe he is just imitating the first male. Anyway, the mantis stack is now tottering, the one in the middle feeling the squeeze. A moment later, the one on top falls off. He tries to get back on while the ride is moving but is unsuccessful. He finally gives up, luckily for him as it soon turns out: the first male keeps riding on the female's back, his tail jerking furiously, until a short while later the female suddenly cranes her head round and bites off the head of her lover! The male doesn't fall off immediately. He keeps hugging the female from behind and his tail keeps twitching. Finally, the female pulls her tail away from his and proceeds to eat the rest of his body, everything except his wings. Her stomach bloated, she slowly walks away.

I stare at the female, wondering whether she has gobbled the male's spirit down into her belly.

Then a frightened ladybird plops onto the windowsill, landing on its back.

With three pairs of legs stuck in the air, it can't right itself. I nudge it with my finger—it retracts its legs and is motionless. I stand a pencil at an angle and put the ladybird on the pencil—it thinks it is on a branch and immediately climbs on up. When it reaches the lead, I turn the pencil upside down. It turns the other way and climbs up to the eraser. After several rounds of this my hand starts aching, and the ladybird shows no sign of giving up. So I put it in a scrapbook I've started making and trace the outline of its body as a souvenir of our time together. I let it go, but it keeps walking through the labyrinth of lines on the paper. Only when I draw a thick shortcut to the edge of the paper does it make an exit.

With the ladybird gone, there isn't anything fun for me to do. I toss aside the scrapbook and crouch on the floor to look for the gecko. I don't find it, but I do notice two suspicious feelers poking out from a hole in the floor. It must be a cockroach! Just then a small insect comes by and the head to which the feelers belong snaps out, snags the insect and instantly retreats into the hole. In that instant, though, I got a good look at him. I get a piece of thread and dangle it in front of the hole. The jaws clamp down on it, not letting go. I pull and find I have fished out a beautiful beetle with twelve stars on its back.

Catching bugs is so much fun. The problem is what to do with them after you catch them, because they never seem to want to play with you. They'll try to escape or play dead. If they fight, they fight for keeps: they won't nibble, just bite.

So I've caught this beetle. I let it nibble on my finger a bit. Chomp! Ouch! What'd you do that for? I want to ask it, but it's already bunkered down in the shadows.

I decide I'd better leave it alone. I lie down in bed and let my mind wander. I start thinking about the Lodge of Braves and all the toys I keep inside.

I designed the Lodge of Braves after seeing a vision in a dream. Inside is all the gear a warrior should have: hunting knife, bamboo spear, pike, bow and arrow, buckskin hat, holster, tunic, quiver and pouch… and there are some toys Grandpa made himself and handed down to me, like a bamboo swoosh, made from ten short sections of bamboo attached by string to one end of a pole. When you turn the pole in your hand, the bamboo sections start whirling above your head. The whooshing sound leaves creatures in the mountain forest spellbound. There is also a blowgun, a long, thin section of bamboo with a projectile that can stun a squirrel at fifty paces. I also have my trophies hung up in there. There are deer antlers, boar tusks, a ram skull, and a complete squirrel skeleton. As I think about these things, my hunting memories start flooding back.

The hardest to catch was the boar, whose attacks were swift and deadly, with teeth that scraped like knives and sharp tusks that could slice your belly open and spill your guts on the ground. But even he could not escape the trap Grandpa and I set for him.

We armed a huge crossbow alongside a boar run. The arrow was really long, and the tip had been sharpened and hardened in a slow burning fire. Then three strips of bamboo with jagged teeth sawn out had been fastened onto the arrow. When the bow was armed, the arrow aimed just below the bait: a piece of caramelized yam. The bait itself was trip wired. When the boar went for the bait, the crossbow shot the arrow clean through his heart.

There was also pit trap that we dug on an animal track and hid with branches and leaves. On the bottom we put bamboo spikes that would impale and immobilize any beast that fell inside. I personally thought this trap was even crueller, that except for a vicious boar no animal should suffer this kind of torture. I had the idea of building a humane trap without arrow or spikes, a pit with a bamboo rack that allows a goat or deer to fall through but catches the antlers, leaving the animal hanging helplessly in midair. I caught muntjacs with my bamboo rack trap and always let them go. Grandpa did not seem pleased. He said letting animals go was not a part of our tribal tradition.

Some of the traps are still set today by disused corduroy roads, some by deserted Japanese rail lines off in the wilderness where human feet now seldom venture. When I visit these places which I have dreamed of, where traps have been set and beasts caught, I find that the animals usually haven't struggled much. There's no sign of resentment, suffering or ferocity. It's like they were pleased to die for me. Sometimes I see their flesh melt right off their bones, leaving their skeletons for me to take home. Grandpa and I still go out hunting, digging pits and setting traps, in my dreams.

I stash everything we catch in my Lodge of Braves, which is actually the only such lodge in or around the village. I keep it hidden under bunches of straw. Father has never found out about it. But not because of me: it's Grandpa who insists that I keep it secret. He is probably scared that the Japanese might find it. I've heard the Japanese destroyed all the lodges in the village. Even though the Japanese are long gone, the old fellow still can't put his heart at ease.

I have another place I keep hidden with straw: the Forbidden Room. The Forbidden Room is on the shore of the stream behind the cabin. It is a small hut I built using twitch grass, rattan and green bamboo. It governs the hunt and the well-being of the tribe. In the past, when tribesmen were sick or needed exorcism, they'd visit a Forbidden Room. In the centre of the room is the Holy Vault, a box made of twitch grass stalks, tough dried vines and arrow bamboo. The Holy Vault can only be opened during a ritual. It is a shrine.

The Holy Vault contains the goddess of the harvest and the hunt. She has a temper and for some reason is fond of squirrels. Grandpa says in her heart a squirrel is the equal of a large boar. Every year come ritual time, Grandpa and I dip cogon grass in water and sprinkle the whole floor of the Forbidden Room with it. Once we have cleaned all the ritual vessels, we fill them with wine and millet. Then we whirl the ritual offering, a string of squirrels, in the air while chanting a prayer of greeting to the goddess of the new year. Grandpa presides with ritual decorum, chanting so softly I can barely hear the words of the prayer. He has warned me that the goddess hates noise and I must take care not to disturb her. The Holy Vault is only opened once a year, when the old goddess is seen off and the new goddess welcomed. I've memorized Grandpa's warning, and whenever I enter the Forbidden Room I am careful not to make a sound. Sometimes when I watch the pile of straw covering the Forbidden Room from a short distance, I see something moving inside. Out might scurry a couple of rats or lizards, or it might just be the wind.

Maybe there is more than a single goddess living in the Holy Vault. In the past after the Japanese destroyed all the ritual huts, the mountain folk didn't bother or were not able to make new ones. I wonder where all those goddesses went. Did all of them move into the Holy Vault behind my house? Wouldn't it get too crowded inside? Sometimes I think they'd just come to visit an old friend, sit down for a rest and a chat and then drift off to some unnamed place.

I've never actually seen the goddess of the Holy Vault appear. I have this bizarre image of her in my imagination: a sorceress with gooseflesh and crane feathers. I hold her image in my mind. But now what are those streaks of light around her? Glowworms perhaps? Or maybe stars? How many are there?

The old crone carries a wicker basket filled with millet. On top of the basket is a knife. She's put the basket beside my bed. Now she produces a bundle of rice straw, lights it, circles it over my head while reciting a spell. When the straw goes out, she puts the charred remainder on the headboard of my bed and stabs the knife through. Then, on the table, she prepares water, leaves of cogon grass, betel nut, pine branches, metal flakes, boar bones and a monkey skull. Before I know it she's blindfolded me and is patting my head with wet cogon grass.

"Dispersed and departed…" comes the voice of the crone through the darkness.

She keeps slapping me with the leaves, front, back, left side, right, while chanting a song in an unknown language, which, like the other songs, I am somehow able to understand.

"The soul of the body remains, but the spirit of the mind

cannot find the way home," replies another voice.

She keeps asking me, "Has your spirit returned yet?"

I am not able to reply, though my memory is gradually returning—

I realize I have drowned and that it happened in a dream. I see myself trying to leap onto a moonbeam but missing and falling into a dark abyss. I plunge into a pool of water at the bottom. I don't have the strength to swim. I am on the brink of giving up.

And then I see a laughingthrush with a snail in its beak and its feet on a stone. It is trying to shatter the snail's shell on the stone and get at the soft meat inside. This scene vanishes, and I see myself again, by the mountain stream behind the cabin. I am sitting on a rotting log Father dumped by the stream. The wood is covered in snails. I am trying to pluck them off. But the log isn't quite as rotten as I thought: it begins to roll! I lose my footing. My head smacks into something as I fall into the water...

"He's back." It is Father's voice. Dimly, I seem to see Grandpa leading the old sorceress away.

I hear a whistling sound, like the wind. The sound is getting louder and louder.

At first it seems like the fluting of a single cricket, then more crickets chime in. Before long it is quite loud. I open my eyes.

Father is standing right by my bed. He is holding a string bag in his hands. When he sees I am awake, he gives me a weary smile and goes outside.

The crickets outside get softer and softer, until the last one stops calling. Father has bagged every last one of them.

Father goes to the stove, quickly washes dozens of crickets, plucks out their innards and sticks in spears of yam and taro. Then he deep-fries the lot of them. The room is filled with a crackling sound and a delicious smell. Soon Father brings over a heaping plateful of fried yam and taro with crispy cricket skin. I give one of them a trial bite. It is as tasty as a live shrimp.

Father tells me to chew each bite twelve times, and goes back to the stove to cook some more praying mantises and grind them into powder.

Later I feel a bit better, though I am not quite myself. Probably part of my recovery is due to Father's mantis powder. But I also think maybe I've been healed by the sorceress. Lucky Grandpa brought her to see me before it was too late.

As I convalesce, Father takes care to nourish me, afraid that I'll get sick again and delay going to school. Every day, there are extra helpings of vegetables, a variety of treats, and every evening the mixed aromas of banana oil and glutinous rice waft from the stove. Father makes these glutinous cakes with leftover ingredients he hasn't used for his breadmen. They taste better than breadmen. Father realizes I like to eat them and I put on weight with them, so he doesn't mind making them for me every day.

After a couple of weeks of lying in bed, I finally return to school. School life is getting more and more monotonous. Me and a couple of classmates usually play together, but they are such wusses! And they're useless at the games we play. They hardly ever win. To be honest, I'm getting tired of it. Sometimes, as punishment, I make them clean the nits out of my hair and the wax from my ears, just as if I were a monkey lord. Then, after school's over, I can't wait to be by myself, in the realm of one in which I am king. I hike up the mountain to gather herbs, or just go home to cuddle Rooster.

Rooster is growing really fast. I can barely find enough bugs to feed him with. He eats all the ones I pluck out of crevices in trees and pecks around on the floor in search of more. Actually he won't lose weight no matter what. He seems to get bigger however much he eats. He would probably gain weight even if he only swallowed the air and the dew. Which is good. But it is a shame that he's got too fat to fly onto the roof and too big and strong for me to hold.

Father has been saying lately that the rooster is already fattened up. One day he goes and feels Rooster's stomach with his hand. A strange expression comes onto his face. He says, "I didn't realize he'd get this fat. Any fatter and he won't be able to walk. I think we should wring his neck in the next couple of days and make something wholesome for you to eat."

He hasn't mentioned wringing Rooster's neck in a long time. Shocked, I say, "Momo, don't kill him. I don't want to eat him."

Father tousles my hair. "You want to keep taking care of him until he's old?"

Then he changes his mind. "Okay, forget it. We won't eat him for the time being."

I think he's seen how well I get along with Rooster and can't bear to see me lose a friend. Then he says, "Look what

I found in the nest this morning." From his pocket he takes out of all things an egg!

"A rooster that can lay eggs!" I joke.

"Roosters can't lay eggs." Father doesn't seem to get my joke.

"So where did the egg come from?"

"I don't know," Father says as he examines the egg. "It must be from someone else's hen."

"But there's nobody living nearby." I take the egg and turn it around in my palm, not finding anything special. "Maybe Rooster's a hermaphrodite?"

"Nonsense. There's no such thing as a hermaphroditic chicken."

I go and pick up Rooster and inspect his backside. Seems normal. He is struggling nonstop so I put him down. Scared out of his wits, Rooster starts tearing around the yard. This seems like it might be fun, so I pick him up again, spank him and release him. After several more rounds of this Rooster gives up and lets me have my way with him.

From the day he finds the egg, Father doesn't mention killing Rooster again. He says we'll keep him until we find out exactly what is going on, but the real reason is he doesn't have any time to deal with the bird. I've been so happy that every day I hunt for insects and leaves to supplement Rooster's diet. And every day I check his nest to see if there are any more eggs.

One day I decide to go to the Enchanted Thicket. In front of the tombstone I speak silently to Grandpa.

"Grandpa, I go every day to see if Rooster's laid any

more eggs. And you know what, there is pretty much an egg a day. Sometimes he's too tired to lay one, but there's at least an egg every two or three days. Father is very pleased. As long as we have eggs, Father probably won't think of eating him. And he knows how to cook sugared eggs for me!"

It is silent in the thicket. The trees seem hoary and magical. There are no buzzing cicadas or calling birds. But suddenly there is a startled caw. A bunch of leaves are shaken down. It is a bit creepy. I swallow my fear and dig up the urn by the tombstone as quickly as I can. I put in a white snail's shell and return the urn to the ground.

"Grandpa, you've told me that a sacred shell is a cowry about two inches across, and that there are three varieties, white, red and black. So far I've just found a white one, but it isn't big enough, and it's from a snail. Does it really have to be two inches across? And what about the Paramount Shell, the chieftain among the twelve Tribal Spirits? It's supposed to be pierced through with holes. Am I supposed to gather all twelve Sacred Shells and choose the nicest one and pierce it? Or am I supposed to find it already pierced?"

I lean against the tombstone, straining to hear. He gives me the answer I deserve.

8
Hiding Out

The days are flying by. There are now two baskets of eggs for me to collect, every day; unfortunately, Rooster doesn't seem to know how to brood properly and sometimes crushes the eggs unless I can get them out in time. So every morning I have to see whether there are fresh ones. If not, I check again at noon, in the afternoon and evening. I have to be careful every minute I am not away at school, in case Rooster lays another egg.

But Rooster just doesn't lay eggs on schedule. At first the eggs appeared at night, but lately there have been eggs during the day too. A moment's lapse on my part and there's another egg in the nest! One day, I decide not to go anywhere. I stand guard by the nest, to see what time the next egg will be laid. But nothing happens all day long. Tomorrow is Sunday. I spend another whole day watching. Nothing. At dawn of the third day, a school day, there is still nothing, so I go to school, coming home at noon to check. (Nothing!) I figure Rooster feels too awkward to lay, being watched all the time. So I change tactics. I hide inside the house at the window so as not to bother him.

The sun gradually moves west. The wind gusts and subsides. I try hard to keep my eyes open so I can see Rooster through the window and a clump of grass outside the window. But my eyelids keep slamming shut. It is only with the greatest effort that I can open them again.

Suddenly there is a clatter outside. I am wide awake.

Rooster is flapping his wings and crowing.

This probably means another egg.

I am about to get up to go out, when I spy something moving at the other end of the clump of grass. I crouch down and ease the window open a little more. All I can see is Rooster going berserk. He has leaped up from his nest and is racing towards the clump. There, a dainty hen appears, poking her head out to greet her passionate boyfriend and looking around to see if the coast is clear.

After they've rendezvoused, they entwine necks and start strolling together around the house, dillying here and dallying there. They disappear for quite a long time around the back of the house before reappearing from the other side.

I patiently wait until dark and tell Father as soon as he gets home. We go to check the nest and—surprise, surprise—find another egg. Father instructs me not to bother the lovebirds. Then he sprinkles more grains than normal around the yard to be sure they both have enough to eat. A week later and the hen is no longer secretive and shy when she comes visiting. She saunters around like a coquette, and even presumes to enter the inner sanctum, lazing in the nest for half the day. Later on she dispenses with the formality of visitation and just moves on in.

Father is very protective of Hen, as if she is a distinguished guest from a distant land. I ask him if he is still planning to kill Rooster. He says as long as there are eggs there is no need to kill him. This just goes to show you how important it is to have friends in high places, even for a rooster.

In taking care of the pair of chickens, I've not had time to worry or do anything about that pair of eyes, though I have been constantly aware of their presence.

But there's one thing I am certain of, and that is that the one hiding outside probably means me no harm and is only interested in the breadmen. I know this because every couple of days I lose a breadman off the windowsill. Based on this fact, I infer that the watcher outside isn't Cub. If it were, why wouldn't she take the breadmen I leave in the hollow of the tree in the Enchanted Thicket? Wouldn't that be easier? Why would she come all the way down the mountain to steal a lousy breadman off my windowsill?

I'm not going to tell Father about the stolen breadmen. For one thing, I'm afraid he'll stop giving me extras. But I also want to play a trick on "it", whoever or whatever "it" is.

First I select the breadman I like best and hide it by my bedside. Then I coat the rest with chilli oil and salt and leave them for "it" on the windowsill.

Over the next couple of days, "it" keeps taking them, despite the taste. But now "it" isn't so carelessly greedy as it was before, taking all the breadmen on the windowsill.

Now "it" is selective, too, taking a single breadman each time, as if it is trying its luck despite repeated failures, as if it still believes there are tasty breadmen for it to take.

The game doesn't actually last very long. A few days later I find out who "it" is. I knew it! It's silly Lotus. It was so obvious: every day after school, she follows Father to where he sets up his stand. She has no money: she never buys any breadmen, she just leans on the stand. Then there was this one time she decided to follow Father home, but on the way Father managed to get rid of her, just by telling her to stay put. She actually did stand still, staring anxiously after Father as he left.

What I don't get is why she's so desperate. Haven't all those spicy breadmen made her sick?

The first time I see Lotus's chubby white hand with the big black mole poking through the window, I am not all that surprised. Actually I feel sorry about what I've done. She's been taking so much trouble to steal a couple of playthings I was going to throw out eventually. And the taste! With the chilli oil and the salt, those breadmen must be a little hard to swallow. Lotus must be feeling pretty miserable. But Father says, no matter what, we cannot give the breadmen away for free, or we'll never see the end of it or of Lotus. Father had indeed given her lots of breadmen, and for ages she wouldn't leave him alone. One day he stopped letting her have any. But what Father doesn't know is that since he stopped giving her breadmen she's been coming to the cabin out of dogged desperation.

From around the time I see her hand I stop covering the breadmen in salt and chilli oil, not wholly because I feel sorry for Lotus, but because I soon discover she isn't the only thief. There is another hand. Some of the breadman-taking has been the work of "the black paw".

Once I see the paw I feel both exhilarated and uneasy. I can't be sure whether it belongs to Cub. But what other animal would follow the scent of the breadmen all the way to the cabin? I open the storybook, the one Momo brought me back from the big city, and look through the animals of the forest, to see which ones have black paws and which might be interested in breadmen. Contradictions well up inside me. Although I become convinced it is a bear's paw, I almost wish it wasn't, because it might not be Cub's.

But one thing is certain: it does belong to a bear.

One night we are woken up by a disturbance outside. We see Rooster beating his wings and screaming. Hen is gone from the nest. In the air float a few feathers and on the ground are several round footprints. Father crouches down to take a closer look. He urges me back into the house. Only after he comes back in and closes the door behind him does he tell me the truth: we've been visited by a bear.

"It's winter now. Maybe it came down to the village because it can't find any food higher up... I've never seen the likes of it. That bear is brave, or maybe foolhardy is a better word for it: it doesn't know how dangerous people can be."

"Did it eat Hen?"

"Yup."

"What about Rooster?"

"I've put him in the shed. He should be safe for the time

being. We should make a coop for him."

"Do bears eat people?"

"Some do, some don't."

I just can't get over it. Why do bears get so horrid when they get big? Is that what will happen to Cub when she grows up? Is that what's already happened to her?

The next day, I trace the bear print on paper and compare it with Cub's. There is a huge difference between them. But what do I know? She's been gone for a long time now. Maybe her paw is now really that big.

Father builds a coop and moves Rooster in along with the eggs. I keep the eggs warm by shining a lamp on them every day, until a brood of downy chicks finally hatches. The chicks look quite unusual. I tell them, "You have your father's feathers and your mother's cluck."

For the past while I have stopped putting breadmen on the windowsill and have been sure to close the window tightly when I go to bed. Lotus can't stick her hand in any more, and neither can "the paw".

But there is no longer any need for Lotus to be sticking her hand in, because Father has gone and brought Lotus home. He gives her breadmen to eat and lets her sit on my magnolia stool. Not that I care. I know her family doesn't love her and she doesn't have any friends at school. Actually, except for getting in the way, she isn't that bad. Like at the temple fair, when I was getting the caged bear's "signature", she covered for me without me having to ask her. She was there when I needed her. Besides, she is obedient, especially to Father. Like that time he told her to stop following him and she really did. She stayed rooted to the spot until dark, when she was discovered by a passing neighbour and taken home. As to why Father's now decided it's okay to bring her here now, maybe he doesn't know what else to do with her. I hear one time Father got fed up, gave her a breadman and told her to stop following him, but it didn't work: she became even more attached to him, scrambling to help him shoulder his load, brush flies and slap mosquitoes away. And she's done lots of nice things for me, too, as if any son of Father's is a son of hers. Wait a minute! That's not quite right: she's only a couple of years older than me—no more than half a dozen—certainly not old enough to be my mother.

I actually don't mind her sitting on my stool, though I do worry about her drooling on it. And Lotus really does have her own special way of eating breadmen. First she licks off the candy colouring, then she gets to the bread filling. Once she's finished eating, Father tells me to take her home. I say Lotus knows how to go home by herself. Father says he will worry and that if she gets lost her family will come looking for her.

Every day, Lotus loyally helps Father carry his load back to the cabin. Father gives her a breadman in return. I wait for her to drool, with a rag at the ready to wipe off my stool. Then I take her home. It's the same routine every day. It's taking up too much of my play time! When Father finds out how I feel, he lets me go and play by myself. I ask what if she gets lost? Father says she already knows the way. What a relief! Truth be told, she knew the way right from the start. Hadn't she come at night to steal breadmen off the windowsill?

A few days later, I don't see Lotus at school. She's gone instead to tend the coop at the cabin. With her there, I can go out to play more often. She is foolish, but she's serious about feeding Rooster and the chicks or cleaning up after them. Her family stopped caring about her a long time ago. They haven't haggled over her wages. Letting her come to my house to do chores is a way for them to be sure she doesn't get into trouble. This way, they don't have to look after her.

And Lotus gets a lot out of feeding the chicks. She has fun doing it. She "draws", by arranging grains of rice in different patterns on the ground. When the chicks peck the grains up, they follow the line of the pattern she's arranged. It is an authentic "birdgraph".

Lotus cherishes every chick as her own. She's very maternal. Every time she feeds them she recites a list of almost a hundred names—there are that many chicks now —and even though they all look alike and her names for them all sound alike, she never seems to make a mistake. When she sees chicken feathers on the ground, she gathers them up and recycles them into a feather corsage or bonnet. She even gave a feather flower to Father and me, even though boys don't wear flowers. I've even seen her doing ikebana on the chickens.

One day the flowers—red, purple, yellow and white —start disappearing off the fence and appearing on the chickens. A brood of chickens decorated with flowers and arranged in a birdgraph on the ground is truly a splendid sight to see, though, it must be admitted, it's a little weird.

9
A Pale Orchid

Returning to the Enchanted Thicket after a long gap, I report to Grandpa on all recent happenings, interesting or not. I also touch up the faded bear drawings on the gravestone. As for the box in the bat tree hollow, it has been a long time since I've stocked it with new supplies. I am happy to find that the food I put in last time has been taken. I put fresh banana cakes and breadmen in the box and put it back.

Cub must be a lot bigger now. I try to imagine her height, build, claws and prints.

If she met me, would she recognize me by sight?

At least she would know me by my smell. There's no way she would miss my smell on the breadmen and cakes.

But is she the hen snatcher? The one who left those round footprints in the yard? Maybe other bears would do such things. But if there are other bears, where are they hiding? Why have I not seen a single bear in the forest?

I can't wait for the next temple fair, but at the same time I'm worried that the tonic hawker won't come. I heard old folks on the plain say that his medicine only worked on the first day and had no effect after that. If nobody wants to buy his medicine, will he and his bear even bother to come?

My days are so dull and tedious. But I don't want to relieve the boredom by being nasty like the boys at school. You know, the kind of boy who pulls up girls' skirts or sneaks into the washroom to watch them pee.

I heard there's been a number of peeping Toms. After school one day, some boys made a human pyramid outside somebody's bathroom window, and then went bragging to anyone that would listen about how they'd seen a naked woman. I am both disgusted and intrigued. I think I might choose a time when nobody is looking and drag a brick over to a window. Standing on tiptoes, my eyes would have their fill. But those boys say that big girls are banshees, who will rip off your trousers and spank you flatter than a pancake if they discover you peeping on them.

There's one girl who wouldn't hit you, though, and that's Lotus.

I heard Lotus has been peeped on lots of times but she never notices. And her house is by the mountain slope, with the bathroom window facing the slope. Usually nobody passes by there, so if you are able to climb the slope you can peep on Lotus without getting found out. But I don't think I would ever watch Lotus bathing, because she doesn't count. At least she doesn't seem like a girl to me, not in that way. Another reason is I don't want to be a bully. I don't want to live on the same planet as people like that.

For some reason, though, Lotus doesn't treat me like we live in the same country, or even on the same planet. To her it's like I am a prince of some fabulous foreign land. She loves to follow me and tread in my footprints, especially down a muddy road.

Who does Lotus think she is trying to fool?

I think it is embarrassing and tell her to stop stepping in my footprints. But she doesn't listen. If she does listen, she makes her own footprints, but she'll still follow me. One time I got so irritated I went and walked behind her and stepped in her footprints, crushing them one by one. Her feet are smaller than mine, so my prints completely covered hers. It looked like only one person had walked down that muddy road: me.

Actually her feet are quite attractive.

I don't know what's going on, but when I look at her feet I have this funny feeling, a feeling I've never had before. I can't help it, it's like a strange new presence.

Those toes so pale and small, that heel so fine and round, her steps are soft and graceful, like a little bird pecking the ground with its tiny mouth.

Secretly I don't mind her walking with me. It's just that I can't let it seem like I "like" her.

And if you don't mind her drooling, she isn't that bad

looking. She is rather nice looking, actually, with a pale oval face, shining eyes, a small nose and a small mouth. I've heard adults use the phrase "a jewel in the rough". That seems right for Lotus. It also seems to me that she shouldn't be called Lotus. Orchid would suit her better. In the forest there is a pale orchid that takes root on tree branches and hangs upside down. You often see clusters of them. If you don't look carefully it looks like vines are growing along the branches; but if you look closer you see the drooping blossoms, light yellow with pale purple spots. Not bad looking at all.

And Lotus has another special skill, boat origami. She can fold a paper boat the size of your fingertip, make a small puddle in the mud with her foot and set the boat afloat. With a favourable wind (supplied by blowing) the boat glides quite nicely.

Sometimes she puts in a ladybird passenger. In a white paper boat a ladybird looks like a streak of silver with an inset ruby glowing in the stream. Rocking gently, the boat might run aground, in which case the ladybird will start to "go ashore", crawling over the hills and dales of Lotus's toes.

Once the ladybird finishes the hike, Lotus says, "You get five points," and gives it something nice to eat. If it fails, Lotus lets it try again, until it succeeds.

"What are you doing?!"

"Playing 'Chaperoning the Ladies on a Journey of Five Mountain Passes'. Do you remember the story about crossing the Five Passes and slaying Six Generals from *Romance of the Three Kingdoms*?"

"Lotus," I say, "what are you talking about?"

Sometimes the ladybird fails to make it over the five passes of Lotus's toes, and instead goes ashore over Lotus's heel. Then she blocks its path with her pretty foot and makes it crawl back onto her toes. When it completes the journey Lotus says, "That's the spirit! Never give up!" I've tried playing once myself. I put the ladybird on my toes, but it immediately jumped off. I put it back on, and eventually it started crawling. But after just one toe, it turned belly up.

"This isn't any fun."

"The ladybird doesn't want to play with you."

This was the first time Lotus had ever made fun of me, but I didn't take it as an insult. It made me realize that she isn't as dumb as she looks.

"I don't want it to play with me." I secretly practise by myself quite a few times, but it's hopeless. Lotus seems to be the only one the ladybirds listen to.

I reveal things to Lotus about Cub. She earnestly promises that she will tell me if she sees her.

But Lotus has never seen Cub before.

Lotus doesn't think this is a problem and enthusiastically helps me look. If she finds a print, she drags me over to show me.

This print in the forest is her latest discovery. I crouch down to inspect it.

"It's probably not Cub's."

"So what kind of print should I look for?"

I motion with my hands. "About this big. With this shape."

She says, "Oh. I've never seen one like that," sounding uninterested.

That peeves me, as if I am the only one who cares about finding Cub. Actually, Lotus is right. She can join or abandon the search just as she likes. She doesn't care about Cub the way I do. Why should she? For her it is just fun, nothing more. She isn't really paying attention, or she doesn't care whether it is a bear print—any print will do. But sometimes she's still irritating. With that earnest tone of voice of hers she seems so eager to please. Lotus runs off ahead and crouches down. She waves for me to come over.

"Is this it?"

Fed up, I don't even look. "No!" She's asking for it.

But she keeps crouching before the print for ages.

This print in the mud is quite deep. There is some water in it, onto which Lotus places a small leaf. She beats the air to make a breeze. The leaf drifts like her paper boat in the shallows. She puts an ant on the leaf, breathes in deeply and blows again. "Bon voyage," she says. In no time the leaf reaches the other shore.

Lotus now seems keen on nothing but ants. I look at her clothing, how it is much too small for her—especially that tight skirt. When she crouches down it doesn't completely cover her bum. I can see the frilly edges of her white panties. And there is a hole in them.

She is always letting people see her underwear like this. That's why people say she is simple. She's actually oblivious, and even if you laugh right in her face she smiles back at you, like you're making fun of someone else.

I always feel sorry for Lotus. I think one day she might

realize what other people think of her and turn into an eagle and fly away forever.

Grandfather told me that the eagle is the reincarnation of a girl of our tribe who was abused by her family. She was always a hard worker but never got a kind word. One day, in despair, she split a dustpan in half and attached the two halves to her shoulders. These halves turned into wings. She became an eagle and flew off with tears in her eyes. Probably, though, Lotus will never know how wretched she is. And when she plays with ants or ladybirds, maybe they seem like her real family.

People are getting ready for the temple fair again. They ask Father to make three tables of mock "offerings". I make the full circuit of the square in front of the temple, seeing no tonic hawkers or people with bears. But there are quite a few entertainers—a monkey tamer, a knife artist and a snake charmer.

The monkey tamer's performance is lively. He doesn't have his troupe of monkeys turn somersaults, jump through rings of fire or ride unicycles like other monkey shows. Instead he's trained them to play the zither and perform *Legend of Lady Whitesnake* with makeup and everything. They really look the part, those monkeys, though the music they play isn't great. As for the acting: when the mystic monk Dharma Ocean matches magic powers with Lady Whitesnake, the monkey in charge of the special effect called "Floods Engulf Goldmine Mountain Temple" is just going through the motions— he splashes a bit of water here and there and goes off to watch the knife artist. As you can imagine, a few splashes are hardly sufficient to submerge Goldmine Mountain Temple, but Dharma Ocean keeps up the act, holding up his magic bowl and incanting the spell to make the waters go back. The monkey playing Lady Whitesnake pays more attention to her wig than to the battle. But the more she adjusts it, the more crooked it becomes. She looks ridiculous.

The knife artist is so good it is frightening. He doesn't cut people or slice his own stomach. He doesn't go on about how sharp his knives are. His thing is cutting flies, and he only cuts flies that have landed on people. He begins by getting a brave volunteer to sit on a wicker chair, one hand wielding a knife and the other shaking out dozens of greenhead flies from a sack. Some start flying off into the blue yonder, others land on the person's face, head and body. With a few flashes of his knife, dozens of dead greenheads hit the ground, including the would-be escapees. Some get blinded or have limbs amputated. These ones fly around a bit before falling. The volunteer hasn't even had time to blink! He gets up and pats himself, but not a hair has been harmed. The crowd claps and cheers and puts lots of money in the artist's hat.

But the most breathtaking act of all is the snake charmer's routine.

The charmer is a young fellow, in his early twenties. His features are delicate, a bit like a girl's. Bare to the stomach, he drapes snake after snake, fangs and tongue exposed, around his head, neck, abdomen, legs and torso. The snakes seem to know what to do. They coil, wriggle and squirm on cue. Every one of them is a garish viper.

With one whistle, however, the snakes fall like rain.

With another whistle, the snakes start rushing to their positions in a "White Sun in a Blue Sky" formation. That's what the charmer says: "Folks, as you can see, there is a sun with twelve rays coming out of it, just like on our national flag!"

Another whistle: the snakes form a bagua trigram, with a yin-yang symbol in the centre.

Another whistle: the snakes form a big arc, stand up on their tails and bow to the audience.

Then the charmer circles the arc of snakes—cobras, tortoise shells, rattlers—opens some of their mouths and sticks his fist in. Those fangs make my hair stand on end. I can't bear to look. Every time he pulls his hand out and shows it to the audience, everyone breathes a sigh of relief.

But there is one person who doesn't bat an eyelid. She isn't afraid of snakes, because she doesn't realize how dangerous they are.

I see Lotus crouching in the crowd, quite near the snake arc. When the charmer is going round with his hat, she goes and pets one of the snakes, which promptly bites her in return. She yelps in pain as the fang wounds blacken and swell. There is a commotion as everyone moves away from the circle so as to get a clear look at Lotus.

The charmer hurriedly applies the antidote, carefully and evenly. Lotus seems to forget the pain and even starts laughing as if someone is tickling her. When he is done, she lifts up her other hand. There are ladybirds squirming on her palm.

Onlookers start laughing. "Will you get a load of that! Lotus tipped him a palm of ladybirds!" "A palm of ladybirds? Like a school of fish, a mission of monkeys or a sleuth of bears?"

The antidote is miraculous. In no time, the wounds stop bleeding and the swelling goes down. People gather round, asking if this medicine is for sale.

What a day! By this time, they've started to distribute the "offerings" in front of the temple. I rush up and somehow get one of the best. I'm disappointed, though, that the tonic hawker hasn't shown up. Someone said he saw him make an appearance in another village. The people there probably knew he was a fraud, but mountain folk being generally decent they didn't expose him. This person said he's switched to selling Monkey Brain Miracle Medication.

"What about his bear?"

"There was no bear, only a monkey."

Only a monkey! I just want to hear about the bear.

Does this mean his bear is never coming back?

10
Chimera

I can't seem to get the tonic hawker's bear out of my mind.

I have a feeling he's been to my house.

He must be the tonic hawker's bear, not Cub.

I think he's also been to the Enchanted Thicket and taken the breadmen from the hollow.

One day at the Enchanted Thicket I catch sight of him and peer at him silently. He is utterly unaware of my existence.

He doesn't know my smell. He is *not* Cub.

Cub must look different now that she's all grown up, but she wouldn't look like *this*.

He doesn't actually look anything like a bear, not like the bears in my storybook. He looks like the tonic hawker's bear. I've seen those ears before. That's it! How could I forget them? When he bent down to take my "offering" I caught a glimpse of his ears. They grew low on his head. The fur on them was thin. I could make out pale skin underneath.

It isn't just the ears. When he steps from the shadows into the sunlight, no part of his body looks right. His thin fur is patchy and unkempt, as if he's just lost a fight, as if he's been on the wrong end of a bite. He's a freak! He has none of the ursine majesty of a bear.

It's him who's been taking the breadmen, banana cakes, candied yams… all those things I've been leaving for Cub!

He's the one who keeps raiding the hollow. But these past few times I've been able to get a closer look at his emaciated paw, a lot like the black paw that has been reaching through the window, but way too narrow to be the hen stealer's.

I trace his print and compare it to the hen stealer's. His is thin, the hen stealer's wide and round: no match. His narrow paws seem to get him off the hook on the charge of hen thievery.

At times, I wonder whether he and Lotus know each other. Or if he followed Lotus to my house. This thought occurred to me because, if he really is "the black paw", he's been stealing breadmen from the windowsill just like Lotus. And he's been standing on tiptoes and watching Lotus bathing, just like the boys at school.

Would a bear copy Lotus?

Do bears like to watch people bathing?

Local people have never mentioned this bear. They know there is something out there, but they think it is a spook.

Once, one of the village boys fell into a stream. His family followed his shouts. When they arrived they saw a bugbear covered in fur pulling him out by the arms. Everybody started shouting and screaming. Only when they threw stones at it and took clubs to it did the creature let the child go and run away.

Another time, a woman was washing her hair at the stream, when suddenly out of the water appeared a furry black wraith. The woman fainted right on the spot. Maybe he really is a bugbear. Personally, I believe he's a bear, not a monster or a spirit. He's just a bear that doesn't look like a bear…

I wonder whether he has met up with other bears. Maybe black bears? Does he have a friend in the forest? Maybe other bears don't recognize him as one of them. But dogs seem to understand him, because they always gather when he howls. He has canine kith but no ursine kin. I am reminded of that evening at the temple fair, of the tonic hawker's whip, of the growling from the cage and of the chorus of barking that followed.

I hope he will remember me like the dogs remember him.

As he has eaten my breadmen, there will come a day when he will know me by my scent.

We seem to have a kind of unspoken understanding about the breadmen in the hollow. Every time I go up there, he always seems to be lurking nearby. Only after I leave does he creep up to take the goods. Then this one time, I discover him hiding not far off between two boulders. I pretend to leave and—lo and behold—he soon sneaks out to check the box. When he turns, I spring from my hiding place. This is the first time we have been so close to each other. This is the first time I've seen him face to face.

With that face, he just can't be a bear. I won't believe it. He isn't a bear, or any of the other animals I can recognize or name. He isn't one of the hundred animals of the forest.

Is he a bugbear?

I am almost scared to tears, but he seems even more shocked than me.

He scoots behind a tree, only revealing a single eye to size me up.

My whole body goes numb. I can't move! Slowly, I get my wits about me and find the courage not to run away. Yes, I am disappointed that my hope has been shattered —it isn't Cub—but at least I have this consolation: even though he isn't a real bear, at least he likes my breadmen.

I show him that in my arms I have a bundled "offering" larger and nicer than what I gave him at the temple fair. The offering is a golden melon.

I am eight or nine steps away from his hiding place. I stop, unwrap the melon and put it on the ground. Then I back away to a safe distance. He appears from behind the tree, slowly walks forward, hesitates as he nears the melon, then bends down and picks it up...

Although I can't see his expression, I am certain he is satisfied with my present, because he takes it after sniffing at it. Then he trots off.

Just as he leaves the Enchanted Thicket, he looks back, as if looking for something. Finally he sees me. Those are the most familiar eyes you've ever seen in your life.

We look at each other across the distance. Time stops on a dark green, windless afternoon. He walks off into the dusk and falls off the surface of the earth.

He might be a wraith or a freak, but he certainly isn't a monster.

Nobody will believe me, but there is one boy who might half-believe—the one who fell into the stream. That boy told me that when he was drowning he felt a force lifting him out of the water. Then he discovered he had returned to shore. The creature only wanted to pull him to safety, not bite him.

Yet, though it didn't do the boy any harm, people still want to catch it and beat it.

The other day a villager was carrying firewood down the mountain, when several branches fell in his path. He heard the sound of breathing behind him. When he turned to look, he saw a bugbear chasing him with a tree branch. He ran down the mountain crying for help. A crowd with clubs came and the creature turned and ran.

Everyone believes it is bad. But I think it was simply trying to help by clearing the path of branches and leaves.

Probably there is one other person who believes— completely believes—and that is Lotus.

One day I saw her holding half a golden melon and asked her where she got it. She gave a silly laugh, took a bite out of the melon and said, "It fell onto my bathroom windowsill." I ask her if she's ever seen a monster.

"What's a monster?" she asks. Suddenly I resent her for being foolish and slow. I feel she just won't understand. Or I don't want her to understand. And at that moment I see a weevil and start trying to catch it, so I don't have time for her silly question.

But Lotus is insistent. "What's a monster?"

The weevil on the tree stump I am staking out takes fright and jumps into a pile of fallen leaves. It draws in its legs and stops moving. I know it is pretending to be dead. I motion for Lotus to shut up and hold my breath as I approach the bug. But Lotus is determined to get a closer look too. Before I can get close enough, the weevil turns over and burrows into the ground.

Awwww! Bother! It had such beautiful shiny green spots.

Lotus knows she's ruined my plan. She says she'll catch another weevil to make it up to me.

"The bugs are all gone. How are you going to catch one?" Ultimately I still look down on Lotus, even though sometimes I think she is all right and am willing to be friends with her. I can't help resenting her for being a nuisance, can I?

I never thought she had it in her. After just a few moments, she's caught a big, gorgeously coloured insect.

"Master..." Lotus presents the bug to me as if it is a precious gem.

I smell an unusual odour and see a yellowish substance on her finger. I know this isn't a good sign and tell her to drop the insect. She does as I say. But the odour remains.

"Stay away! That was a stinkbug." I keep my distance. Lotus sniffs at her hand. Wanting to get the smell out, she starts wiping her hand vigorously all over her clothing. But that only makes things worse.

I tell her to stop wiping and take her to find water.

"What is this monster you were just talking about?" Lotus repeats her question along the way.

"Don't you know about monsters?"

"No. Where are they?"

"I was just fooling. Monsters are imaginary. They don't exist." I can't explain and decide not to say anything more.

From up in the trees a bird calls. It is a high-pitched fluty sound. I look up into the canopy and catch a glimpse of a tiny form.

"Yellow-bellied bush warbler," I say.

There is another bird call, clear and crisp yet sorrowful: *hway hway hwai–yooooo.*

Lotus looks up and birdwatches with me, cupping her ears. "What's that one?"

"White-eared thrush."

Kee kee kee, a sharp throaty sound. I say it is a woodpecker's call.

Birds are calling from all over the leafy canopy. Lotus finds it hard to pin down the sources, because different birds are crying at the same time, sometimes calling back and forth as if in answer to each other. I listen carefully, as if I am trying to catch a number of fleeting breezes all at once.

There is a delicate *jah jah jah-jah* sound. "Red chickadee," I say quickly.

Gee gee gee… Similar to the throaty sound. "Grey-wing laughingthrush."

A hoarse staccato sound: *guh guh guh guh-iee-o.* "Formosan tree pie," I say immediately. Then there is a metallic sound: *meeeee-do re-meeee.*

I gulp. Lotus asks what it is. "White-tailed robin."

"How do you know so much?"

"My grandfather taught me."

"You've got a grandfather? Why haven't I seen him?"

"Of course I have a grandfather. You haven't seen him because he lives far away, way up there in the sky."

Lotus looks up at the sky, a baffled expression on her face. "How come he doesn't fall down?"

"He won't fall because he is a celestial being. Don't you know anything?" I say, and turn to walk away.

Then I hear from behind me a burst of sound.

Lotus asks me if I know what it is. I turn around to look at her and say, "That's an odd bird call. I don't know."

"It's a hen." Lotus beams at me and does it again.

"Cluck cluck cluck, cluuuuck cluck cluck."

It really sounds like a hen. I tell her to do it again. She calls again, but this time she sounds like a chick.

Finally we find a pond. The water is dark and forbidding, with muddy bubbles. The bubbles keep welling up to the surface but don't burst. But I have no time to worry whether the water is clean or not: I make Lotus jump in while I stand at a distance, breathing sighs of relief.

Lotus stays in the water for a long time, until the stinkbug smell is gone. But when she comes out of the water there is another smell on her, like dead fish or rotting grass. I'm not sure which smell is worse.

"All you had to do was wash the smell off. Why did you stay in so long?!" I don't want to feel this way, but it's like her foul smell is rubbing off on me. Lotus extends her hand. In her palm are several translucent spheres, insect eggs. I ask how she got them and she takes me to the pool. There are several water bugs skimming the surface. They have eggs packed closely on their backs. One time I saw a female insect laying eggs one by one on a male's back and wings. Then the male swam all around with his precious burden, as if trying to keep away from any egg snatchers. This kind of water bug rarely surfaces, so this water must be really foul.

"Look! You've stunk out even the stinkiest bugs." Actually, water bugs aren't stinky. I just say this to annoy her. Lotus isn't angry, though. She never throws tantrums and doesn't understand why people get angry at her.

The eggs are really pretty. I appreciate the thought. But what am I supposed to do with insect eggs? Incubate them until they hatch into grubs? In Lotus's hands, the eggs will break sooner or later, so I tell her to return them to the male. As she doesn't know which male she got them from, all we can do is divide them equally, putting one on each male's back.

"Lotus, don't catch insects or insect eggs for me again, okay?" I don't want her to feel she owes me anything, much less mess things up. She nods obediently, though the disappointment shows on her face. She must be thinking, "Now I've gone and done it again."

To console her, I say she hasn't done anything wrong,

and to make her feel better about herself I teach her two of my special skills.

My first special skill is scarab beetle appraisal.

I catch several large scarabs and turn them over on their backs to inspect the lines on their bellies. The number of lines tells you the rank of the scarab. The alpha male has eight golden lines.

"This one is powerful. It can fly a long time."

One only has two lines.

"This one is flighty and impetuous. It flies all over but doesn't get far."

Lotus practises "the method" a couple of times. She seems to get it.

Then I teach her my other skill: spider fighting.

I use a kind of spider warrior called a turquoise spider, whose body is only the size of a fingernail. They like to make dens by the wayside, with lots of rooms in each den. The entrances to the dens all have "front doors", covers of silk with fine sand sprinkled on top. Inside there are passages connecting the rooms together. As soon as they discover an intruder they flee to another room and close the "door" to block the way.

The den of the turquoise spider is deep, and carefully decorated inside. There is silken wallpaper in every room. The very end of the den is sectioned off for the bedroom and the bathroom. Most of the time, they lie in wait for prey under the cover over the entrance. When something edible passes by the gate, they pop their heads out and drag it in.

I start teaching Lotus to poke a cover away from the

entrance of a turquoise spider den. But the spiders are afraid of exposure. Whenever Lotus pokes the cover, the spiders on the other side pull it back into place. She tries several times before she manages to dislodge the cover and turn it over. The resident spiders are hanging on the other side. "Turquoises are naturally fierce and cruel. If you ever get tired of crickets, all you have to do is catch a few turquoises, put them in a glass jar, and they'll fight to the death. And they do it in style; they're beautiful little creatures, and they look even better when fighting." That's how I describe to Lotus the amusement I get from my second special skill.

But Lotus doesn't seem to like spider fighting. Uncovering the dens seems like more than enough fun for her. She has no other tricks up her sleeve. Then I tell her that turquoise spiders taste sweet, just like honey, and Lotus immediately pops one in her mouth and starts chewing. But then she immediately scrunches up her brows and says, with the most comical expression on her face, "It's sour!" That doesn't stop her from uncovering other spider dens and trying other turquoise spiders. But each one is just as sour as the last.

Though Lotus doesn't like sour insects, she is surprisingly fond of stinky ones. She likes tumblebugs, also known as dung beetles. She can detect the camouflage over their burrows and scoop out the stash of faeces that the tumblebugs have so laboriously gathered. She puts these precious golden-brown balls in a glass jar for appreciation, and sometimes she even donates them to charity, giving "ready-made" balls of dung to other tumblebugs to take home for their hungry little tumblebug children. Lotus seems to be the Robin Hood of the Insect Realm, but maybe all she's doing is stealing shit from its rightful owners and depositing it somewhere else, so that the owners have to push it home again. It seems like a pointless exercise, and I can't imagine the tumblebugs think it is much fun.

11
A Canine Chorus

I believe Lotus doesn't know the creature, whatever he, or "it", is. I also believe the creature is fond of Lotus. More than once he has moved a stone near her bathroom window so he can watch her bathing by moonlight. He doesn't even try to avoid running into me. (I've been following him.) Perhaps he doesn't feel he is doing anything wrong. As for me, when I hear those machine gun bursts and slow sloppies coming from Lotus's bathroom window, I have to run away, covering my mouth to suppress my giggles.

I often meet him at the Enchanted Thicket. I've started calling him "Kody". When I call "Kody", he knows I am talking to him. He runs over and replies, "*Wuuuuaaaaah.*"

Looking carefully, I see he is half-boy, half-bear. Except for *URSINE BILE MIRACLE MEDICATION* there are no other words he can write. Perhaps he doesn't even know what writing is. His palms are not like animal paws, even though they are covered in dark fur. They are thin and clawless.

I take Kody to Grandpa's grave and tell him the story of how Grandpa became a bear. I exaggerate a bit, turning Grandpa into the Celestial Spirit himself rather than just his Guardian.

Kody may not understand human language, but he must understand the drawings on the gravestone. I use pebbles and muddy ruddle to touch up Grandpa's story on the stone. I also imitate the temple fair ritual and place sacrificial offerings (fresh breadmen) before the gravestone.

Kody seems to realize the solemnity of these gestures. He calmly watches the ritual and doesn't make a nuisance of himself.

I dig up the urn by the gravestone, open the seal, and carefully count the shells. "These are Sacred Shells, our most precious tribal possession. Each shell is the abode of one of the Tribal Spirits, so we must be especially careful with them. Usually the Sacred Shells must remain in this urn under the protection of the ancestors. Every year we hold a ceremony in honour of these spirits. These shells can walk and fly, and they practise the art of invisibility to avoid being taken by scoundrels. They return to their original form in the presence of decent people. Sometimes they are mischievous and shy, but if you're nice, and you're willing to wait long enough, you will see them in their true aspect. In all the world there are only twelve Sacred Shells. I have found eleven of them. One more and the set will be complete." Even if Kody doesn't necessarily understand, in his eyes I see reverence.

I rustle up a taro leaf, a tree branch, a gourd and a pile of firewood.

Lighted, the branch is a torch. Split, the gourd is a ready-made drinking vessel. I pile up the firewood to make a pyre. Reenacting a scene I saw in a dream, I start to conduct the ritual. I serve as Ritual Master, while Kody acts as Acolyte.

In my left hand I hold the burning brand, in my right a hunting knife. Kody crawls on the ground, his hands grasping my ankles. I begin by silently praying, then shout up at the sky, "Descend, O Ye Tribal Spirits." The whole forest changes into a mansion, which tribesmen enter from all around. We light the pyre. Twelve tribesmen hold human likenesses made of straw; forming two lines, they face each other across the fire, singing alternately, to answer each other. At the climax of the song they toss the straw figures onto the pyre. This is their song:

i likihli likihli iui i lavahli lavahli
ina muli vengeeli iui mulilalee vuai
ina mataru taruuhl iui matalalee vuai
ina hlisapeta vinau i saramarukaruka
ina vengavenga vihluua i kupatarahlapee
kupatarahlapee kumiakui iaiai

The spleenwort fronds in moonlight clear the fog,
And flames are dancing on a ribwood log.
Our patewood cups are filled with mead and grog,
Beneath the routbaum roasts a feral hog.

Next, I spread out a deerskin on the ground, on which a flesh offering is placed. Wine is poured into a vessel, and I, as Ritual Master, use my finger to drip wine over the offering. Once the offering is consecrated, I lift a boar tusk and a knife in one hand and hold Kody's hand in the other. The host of tribesmen touch the clasped hands of the Ritual Master and the Acolyte as a pledge of spiritual unity. Then I remove the Sacred Shells from the urn and put them on the taro leaf, sprinkling over them a rooster's blood. The white Sacred Shells are instantly dyed red. Then wine is dripped to return them to white. The Ritual Master gathers the Sacred Shells back into the urn, buries it in the ground again, and finally leads the host in a dance around the pyre.

Hlamatakupuhlainaia inacalihlana ahlupu ia
anikiakikihla patulu patulu pavau pavau

As I conduct the ceremony, I explain the chant to Kody. The story happened long, long ago. A hunter of the tribe of Hlamatakupuhlainaia delayed the hunt because he was reluctant to leave the bedside of his beloved. When he returned, his fellow tribesmen were unforgiving. So he turned into a sorrowful eagle circling the mountain valleys, forever scouting out prey for the brothers of Hlamatakupuhlainaia.

I repeat the song to Kody, and he hums enthusiastically. A canine chorus chimes in.

*Hlamatakupuhlainaia inacalihlana ahlupu ia
anikiakikihla patulu patulu pavau pavau*

*Brothers of Hlamatakupuhlainaia hunt there
and hunt here,
To the east run the boar to the west run the deer.*

This is the moment of greatest holiness for Kody and me. Kody has been accepted into the tribe.

But there are those outside the forest who do not acknowledge Kody's membership in the tribe or any human community. They see him as a calamity. They harass and hound him. When he has nowhere to turn, I try to help him. I take him back to my house. But as soon as Father sees Kody he grabs an axe.

Kody flees out the door as I hold onto Father, not letting him chase after Kody.

"Momo, he's not a monster. He isn't."

Father is exasperated. He flings me aside and charges out, saying, "If it's not a monster, then what is it?"

"He's a bear," I cry.

Father ignores my begging and my sobs, throwing me on my bed and bolting fast the wooden door of the cabin. I decide to make a clean break. I wait until the middle of the night, when Father is fast asleep. I climb out the window and run and run, running until I am as far away as far can be.

I reach the summit of the mountain. It is blowing hard: a sea of trees howls as the moist air sweeps over it. My face covered in tears, I hoot and holler in all directions. The wind drowns out my voice. In spite of this I take a deep breath and bellow. My bellow causes the howling wind to pause! My echo bounces around the valley: there is now no other sound.

But suddenly I feel afraid. For quite a while I stand there motionless, moving only my eyes to survey the surroundings. It is a night of wind and cloud. The moon keeps appearing and vanishing. In the distance there are only a few lights here and there. I am at the edge of a steep hill. I stand there for a time, watching the lights go out one by one. Nobody's likely to come after me, I think, as nobody yet knows I have left. But what good will leaving like this do? Now I seem to be worried that nobody will be able to find me.

I find a small cave away from the wind and put leaves inside. There is barely room enough to squeeze my body in. The air is icy, much colder than I expected. Slowly I feel my scalp go numb. Passing insects know well enough to leave me alone.

Sparse stars are shining silently in the night sky. At first glance the light of the stars seems white, but looking again you see it isn't a pure white; it is tinted with silver, light gold, crystal blue and pale orange. The stars seem to be slowly wandering, changing formations, gliding towards the moon.

In the starlight, my surroundings are dark and foreboding. The trees are black silhouettes. It seems that water should be flowing and insects moving, but there is almost no sound. It is too quiet. The whole world seems to be sleeping. I close and open my eyes. The minutes creep by. For the longest time I don't think about Kody or about Father. I just listen to the sound of my breathing. Everything else becomes insignificant. When I finally fall asleep, there is no mystery or fantasy in my dreams. My mind follows the clouds in the sky as they gather and disperse.

The next day at dawn I wake up in a sea of cloud and birdsong. The mist has vanished. The view is brilliantly clear. Giant evergreens wear a plumage of needles. There are also silver birches, mountain oaks, red maples and cypresses—all these have changed colour, stitching a patchwork autumn tapestry. I get up and wander around to enjoy the miraculous sights, and sounds.

There is the gurgling sound of the creek. The crinkling sound of the leaves.

The sound of birds flitting in the trees. The sound of insects crawling.

The sound of ripe fruit falling to the ground.

I close my eyes and keep moving forward, pretending not to see. The vast mountain forest makes sure I do not go astray.

I cover my ears and carry on by smell.

The wind leads me in all directions. Is that the smell of sun-baked earth? In their simplicity, the odour of mud, the fragrance of fruit, the perfume of plants and the scent of birds and animals seem incomparably lovely.

"Kid, you up here alone?"

A beekeeper passing by with a hive on his back turns his

head and greets me.

I've seen this man before several times, but I've never replied to him. I can never remember what he looks like. He has no fixed abode. His thin body makes you feel he is very much alone. I never see any other beekeepers in the mountains. He is working out of season—I don't know where he thinks he can find flowers now. But his steps are quick and firm and from his expression he seems self-assured. For the first time, I ask a question in reply:

"Old-timer, you by yourself?"

He stops and looks at me again. I can see his face clearly but he still doesn't give me a lasting impression.

"Yes. Have you seen anyone else in your alpine travels?" His voice is loud, but it is as if he is speaking from the other side of a mist.

I say, "I haven't seen any other passers-by. It's just me."

"What are you doing here?" the old-timer asks.

"Looking for something," I say.

"What are you looking for?"

"An old companion."

"Have you found him yet?"

"Nope."

No, I haven't found who I'm looking for. Sometimes I lose hope.

I want to find Cub.

I hear the chickadees chirping from far off, the squirrels scuttling along the branches, even the faint sound of ladybirds spreading their wings. But I don't hear the sound I want to hear: Cub's approaching footsteps.

She's probably grown big by now. Wouldn't her heavy

body moving through the forest make a sound or leave a trace?

I beg the beekeeper to let me be his companion and hunt for sources of pollen and nectar with him. I am not really that interested in the pollen and nectar. I have other fish to fry. But if I could find a source of pollen and nectar, I think, that would be just like finding honey. And there's no bear that doesn't like honey…

"Finding a source of honey isn't just looking for flower blossoms. You've got to judge the terrain, season and weather." The beekeeper knows the locations of the productive flowers like the moles on the back of his hand. He's already scouted out a few routes. Today he is following these routes to find a feeding ground for his bees.

I've almost never travelled with a stranger before. I look him over again and feel he is no longer so strange and mysterious, just a bit hard to work out. We are walking together clear as day, but he still seems far away. I touch the hive lightly with my hand to give myself a sense of reality.

The hive looks really old, as if it might come apart with one yank. I ask him, "How many years have you had this for?"

"Decades."

Decades? I take yet another look at his appearance, and he starts seeming older and older. But bees can't live for decades and decades. He must have gone through several generations of bees already.

"How long does a bee live?" I ask.

"At the most three months, at the least only one." The

beekeeper explains that in an abundant season, the bees fly their hearts out to hundreds of blossoms every time they are let out. The endless work takes its toll; they are short-lived.

I try to imagine what that would be like. Like Grandpa slinging a pouch, the bees would fly out of the hive looking for pollen and nectar, storing the nectar in their crops. If a bee got hungry on the return trip, the only thing to eat would be what was in the crop. His crop empty again, he'd have to fly back for more. If he got hungry again with so much flying, a vicious cycle would soon form. No wonder he would exhaust himself and die young.

"If they fly too far and can't get back immediately and they've got nothing to eat, would they eat what they've gathered?" I want to see if my theory is right.

"No. They know their duty. They'd sooner endure death than touch what's in the crop."

I never thought bees would die of hunger in order to fulfil a sacred mission. But then I haven't seen any dead bees along the way. At this time of year there aren't many sources of pollen and nectar. It should be harder for them to find food now—if they really die from work or hunger like the beekeeper says, why don't I see some fallen apiarian warriors? I suddenly wonder whether there is a Cosmic Bee to guide their spirits by the light of the moon to the mountain heights.

I ask the beekeeper what happens to bees after they die.

"Nobody knows. When they get old and feel they're nearing the end, they will go off by themselves to a place only they know." From the look on his face, it almost seems he is talking about himself.

I ask him where he lives.

"In a forest grove."

"What would you do if the flowers failed to bloom?"

"I'd take my bees and go somewhere else."

Listening to him I have a sense of sadness, thinking him the most lonely person in the world, but also feeling a certain awe, like he is a spirit. I suppose if there was only a single Celestial Spirit up in the sky, the Spirit would get lonely too.

The beekeeper comes to a flat field by a slope and puts down his hive. He opens the eastern entrance to the hive and sets up a crude awning.

Then he looks up at the sky and says, "You should go home. Kids shouldn't be out by themselves so long."

"But I want to see you let out the bees." I sit on the ground, unwilling to get up.

His expression changes, and he orders me to leave in an old and growly tone. Yet I see in his eyes a slyness in his sternness. The sternness is due to his dignity, while the slyness tells me he suspects I might not listen. He spoke to me in this way to give me a bit of a scare, not to be nasty.

I start running, to where the beekeeper can't see me. I run up the slope to find a hidden observation post, but when I look down all I can see is the awning. There is no sign of the keeper or his hive.

A sweet fragrance wafts over. I hear a faint buzzing. I look around but can't see where it's coming from. I jerk my head around again to see the beekeeper appear behind me. He is moving slowly. Then he vanishes into a dense thicket. I look around another time. Now the awning has vanished too.

Caw! Caw! Caw!

A crow is shrieking as it flies overhead. A sheet of dark cloud is approaching. Suddenly frightened, I cover my head and run. Now there is nobody to tell me how long I can stay out alone. Over the ground a gust of wind sweeps fallen leaves onto me, like a million buzzing bees. I struggle to keep running, but wave after wave of leaves attacks me, until I jump into a pool and give those devils the slip.

Maybe I've wished to meet with a spiritual being or Grandpa, but the beekeeper is neither, I'm sure of that.

I don't dare follow the beekeeper. I would rather hide in the shade by the pool for a while. Probably I just ran too quickly, because now I feel weak and hungry, though I'm not in the mood to go and find something to eat. What is there to eat anyway? I try not to think about my stomach, but can't help fantasizing about star anise chicken wings, roasted boar, steamed banana cakes. Then I realize I am actually smelling real banana cakes! I look around and find a whole crate of them in a deserted cottage hidden in a clearing in the woods. As there is nobody around, I take the lid off the crate and see it is full of big golden cakes in the shapes of different animals: pigs, turtles, bears and dogs. I can't decide which one to eat first. Then I hear the sound of footsteps outside. I hurriedly stick the cakes into my sack, thinking I might as well stock up on as many meals as I can. But as I am doing so a cloud of flies reaches me, wanting to join in the fun. I swat flies with one hand

and grab cakes with the other. More and more flies arrive, and all the cakes in the sack fall out onto the ground.

I feel a hand helping me shoo away the flies. Then the flies are gone. The smell of banana cakes is now even stronger. The footsteps disappear. I open my eyes, realizing it was only a dream. Or was it? Right in front of me are several fresh banana cakes placed upon a clean taro leaf, which was lying on the grass beside me as I slept. There are flies buzzing around the cakes and right at the tip of my nose.

There is no cottage in the trees, though the cakes must have come from some human house somewhere, from one with a stove. Have I been discovered? If so, why hasn't my discoverer woken me and taken me home? Perhaps he is afraid I'll just leave again and go even further away.

12

Some Things You Never Forget

First a beekeeper, now a herbalist. When he twists a blade of grass in his fingers, he seems to be speaking, like a gust of wind through the grass and leaves. But when you ask him something, he just stands there like a block of wood. The wind stops, the trees quiet: there isn't a sound in the world.

I meet him on the mountain. I've always felt this mountain belonged just to me, for apart from the beekeeper I've never seen any other people up here.

One end of a long rope is attached to his body The other end is fastened above. He is swinging across the face of a sheer slope. There is a knife slung on his hip. I yell at him, asking him what he is doing. He says he is looking for herbs.

Herbal medicine. I get it. Grandpa taught me to tell certain herbs apart. But when I get a chance to look I don't recognize any of the medicines in this herbalist's sack.

The herbalist tells me, "The herbs that people have never seen and that grow where people have never been have the best medicinal properties."

I say I don't understand how this can be.

He explains, "Medicines today are getting less effective. Illnesses are harder to fight. I've picked all the good medicinal herbs at lower altitudes. Now I have no choice but to climb up here."

I still don't understand, but he has already swung out of earshot.

The herbalist seems to have found nothing on this stretch of slope, so he finds an outcropping, tugs his rope down and flings it further along. Swaying off a precipitous slope, he seems calm and comfortable, like he was born up there as a clump of grass. Occasionally he'd get blown or rained on a bit, but that's all.

The herbalist is higher now. The clouds seem to turn around him. He is so high up I can't see him for ages. All I can see is a strange clump of grass in the air, tall and thin —now it's getting bigger and bigger. And there is a strong, unidentifiable smell. It makes me giddy, but is at the same time soothing. I call up to the herbalist several times. His voice comes from right and left, from above and below. I seem to be floating gently in a kind of flickering light, no longer feeling the weight of my own body. I am unable to move.

When the herbalist comes back down, I ask what he's just been gathering. He shakes his head and slaps the dirt off. "The herb I'm looking for is like a hermit that won't leave his cave. I won't force it."

He shows me the medicine in the sack and teaches me to recognize some herbs. He even takes me to find some, and tells me about the wide range of medicines. Not all of his medicines are herbs: the herbalist crouches by the path, scrapes away a spider's web and teaches me how to treat a wound with it. I learn quickly. He stands up, collects his rope and knife and tells me, "You really should go home now. Don't linger out here too long." Just like the beekeeper. Then, hoisting the sack on his back, he leaves.

He walks so quickly! I follow him with my eyes, then, silently, with my legs. He walks along the bottom of the slope, where the sun can't shine on him. His shadow is layered over the shadow cast by the ridge above, as if he has no shadow at all. His steps are firm and from behind he doesn't look in the least bit old. But there is this sense of solitude about him, as if he's always been as lonely as he seems now.

Discovering I haven't gone home yet, the herbalist calls out to me and lets me walk beside him. He teaches me an interesting game.

It is a unique way of playing the whistle. He's seen me playing my willow whistle the normal way; now he shows me how to play it the other way round. The sound isn't like when Father, Grandpa or I play it. It is a strange sound, unpleasant. But a cicada in the tree actually replies to it with a faint pulsation.

The herbalist has me crouch and play with my lips pursed. This sounds even worse, dull, like a stifled fart.

"What's the point of playing it like this?"

He says, "Look on the ground."

A black dot is making its way over.

I keep blowing and the dot starts jumping. When I stop it stops too.

"Look, the flea is dancing!" The herbalist gives a queer laugh, like the call of a muntjac in April. He takes the willow whistle and shows me some other ways of blowing. One way makes the flea jump high, another makes a pair of fleas take turns jumping, while other ways command a flea to leap high or low, to hop forward or back.

I don't know how he learned this game. Maybe he isn't as lonely as I think. Someone must have taught it to him, right? Or maybe he is really that alone, and that's why he invented these tricks, to make his loneliness easier to bear. When I ask him to make the cicadas call, he blows, softly. But then we hear the clamour of birdsong, which drowns out the cicadas. Next thing I know the herbalist is gone.

I wonder if that beekeeper and herbalist might actually be Grandpa's incarnations. Or his messengers? Like Grandpa, they are both old, alone and of no fixed abode. Their features give you a vague impression, like they are figures in a dream. And they have miraculous skill. I asked Grandpa about it one night, but got only snores in reply. I shook him awake and made him tell me. He took me to a huge hive hidden in a thick grove, but ordered me not to go near in case I disturb the queen. Then he took me to the edge of a very steep drop. Out of a spider's nest grew a strangely shaped and strongly scented herb. Every leaf like a fantastical whistle, the plant made different sounds depending on the direction of the wind.

The sun has just set behind the top of a densely wooded valley. The hills are bathed in twilight. The curtain of night is falling. The shadows of the hills are hiding the trail home. Though in my heart I have wavered, I am now set on remaining here.

It is dark now. My hunger is hard to endure. I walk into the trees to look for that abandoned work shelter, built by camphormen in Japanese times. Maybe Grandpa slept here when he was logging camphor. It's certainly possible. At any rate, I know inside I'll find a brick stove, a square table, a couple of stools, a pile of partly burnt logs as well as branches and kindling. When I get there the floor is a mess, as if a cyclone has blown through.

I can't find anything to eat, just a few empty containers, peanut shells and mouldy provisions. Luckily I manage to find some tools, cut some firewood and dig up a couple of tubers, which I take back to the yard to cook.

In the firelight, the trees around the shelter look spooky. There is the occasional crackle of pine branches, but there is also this other, indistinct sound, like a rustle of leaves.

I raise a torch for protection, go inside and close the door. Looking out through the window, I see there is indeed a shadow in the yard, moving slowly.

It stops a dozen steps away and looks in. Suddenly the huge form stands up straight. I see claws raised high in the air. I feel a sense of dread.

But it doesn't charge at me. It approaches slowly, coming closer, closer.

Finally it stops. Its flared nostrils sniff the air, its eyes watch me silently, in them a gloomy and yet stubborn glimmer, which vanishes in the darkness. Then it turns and disappears.

Finally. We have met again. It was Cub.

Cub isn't a cub any more, but I could never forget those eyes.

Cub has grown up into an adult bear, into a mighty sow.

Are my lucky stars shining particularly brightly? Or did Grandpa hear my prayer and arrange for Cub to find me? No matter what, I cannot let Cub leave me again.

I follow the droppings, prints and claw marks on tree stumps. Tracking her might be dangerous, but I want to see Cub again. Even if she is now a vicious killer who steals hens, I want to see if she still knows my scent.

Cub knows I am following, but doesn't attack, run away or approach. Her steps are quick and agile. Her round body passes easily through the woods, without disturbing a single leaf or twig. Every step seems exact and just right.

I keep my distance, watching her. She seems not to mind. This way I can understand her lifestyle, sound and movements.

When she shouts *Awwooooo*, that means she is laughing.

When she makes a *Rrrrr-gaw rrrrr-gaw* sound like she is clearing her throat, she is sending a friendly message.

When she raises her lips and puffs hard, that means she is uneasy or anxious.

When she flattens her ears and bares her teeth, she is telling you to get lost.

Cub moves swiftly through the forest, stopping sometimes to sniff around. If she finds a place to her liking, she scrapes her claws over the bark of a tree trunk. Or she'll just urinate on the base of the tree, like a dog.

When she stashes food, she makes a nest nearby as a marker and to ward off other animals. She has nests and dens everywhere, sometimes a hollow in a tree or in a rock wall, sometimes made out of leaves and branches. After she eats, she likes to lick her limbs and tummy. When she wakes up, she always scratches herself all over, rolling herself in a ball with her front paws for her back and her hind paws for her chest. If that isn't enough, she'll rub her back on a stone wall.

Yes, Cub is still Cub, just too big for me to carry. But I can still tickle her.

I take out my willow whistle and give it a try. Amazingly, black specks begin moving on her body. When I change my tune the specks throb all together.

At first, Cub—I suppose I should call her Bear now that she's got so big—is intrigued by this game. As I play she walks around me and watches as the fleas come out. She looks uncomfortable. A new rhythm seems to make her eardrums itch. She can't stand it: she starts jumping around.

I never imagined there would be so many fleas in her soft black fur. I want to invent a way of playing that will make all those fleas flee, but no matter how I blow the fleas keep jumping in place. The harder I blow the higher they jump. And Bear starts leaping in the air or rolling around on the ground even more desperately.

I stop playing, to give Bear a chance to find a stone wall to rub her back against. At one point, Bear seems to forget her itchy misery and rambles around the woods like nothing has happened. She still doesn't mind me watching and lets me follow her at a short distance.

But where is Kody?

I go to the Enchanted Thicket several times and manage to find some grub to put in the box in the hollow. But Kody never touches it.

Maybe he hasn't come. Maybe he is afraid of people.

Or maybe he only wants to eat sweets.

I can't give him sweets. I am exhausted and starving myself. And I can't bear to leave Bear, having found her again after so much time.

One day Bear goes into another mountain hut—could it belong to the beekeeper or the herbalist? Or to a hunter? —and doesn't come out for a very long time. I can't wait any longer, so I go in after her. Bear has wreaked havoc. There are crumbs and stains everywhere from broken bottles and empty tins.

I walk through the back door and find Bear sleeping in the hollow of an enormous tree. She reeks of booze.

It has never occurred to me that Bear might drink, and to the point of getting drunk! But that doesn't mean she likes to drink. Maybe she is curious or truly thirsty. I wait by the tree two whole moonlit nights. She doesn't wake up even once, like she has gone into hibernation. And there isn't anything left to eat.

The soil up here is barren, at least of yams and potatoes. I dig as hard as I can, but don't find a single yam or potato. I've found and cooked all the yokebugs in the grass and cicada grubs in the earth. There should be nuts and seeds stashed in a hollow by some woodpecker. I hunt from tree to tree and eventually find two such stashes and gobble them down. I've exhausted all the sources of food in this habitat that a human could eat.

I try to uproot some grass and ruminate on it, but I have to spit it all out after a few chews.

I sit there dazed in the sun, watching a bunch of strangely coloured butterflies, scarabs and rhinoceros beetles crowding on an ooze of sap. They seem to be starving too.

I am fainting from hunger. I sit under the tree and try to doze. But I just can't. Then I see something moving in the distant woods.

Monkeys!

I follow them. There are two monkeys high on a tree trunk picking fruit. One is big, the other small, like a mother and child.

They are tossing these small red fruits into their mouths, glancing down at me. They pick so quickly they almost don't have time to swallow, let alone chew. They are stuffing themselves nonstop, until their cheeks bulge. I wait quietly beneath the tree, not having the strength to climb up and join them. I don't know what to do. Maybe throwing stones would help. No, I'll just wait for the monkeys to come down.

At last they are ready. They keep their eyes fixed on me as they creep cautiously down.

A young one crouches on the ground, eyeing me, as if he is going to attack me like an alpha male. But he is too small. I bare my teeth and he scurries away.

His mother isn't afraid of me, though. She chews as she strolls along, using her hand to massage her bloated cheeks as she spits out yellow seeds one by one.

My eyes are red with hunger. The monkey mother is flaunting food. I can't stand this kind of teasing. I bound up to her and copy the posture of an aggressive male. I glare at her, crouching down and revealing my teeth.

At this the mother is flustered. She takes on a battle posture as well and prepares to meet me.

I bawl at her a couple of times, and she screams at me. As she screams the fruit in her mouth starts falling out. We keep this up until I pick up a stone and threaten her with it. She runs away in panic.

Relieved, I pick up all the pieces of fruit in the grass, like I've swindled someone out of precious jewels and the victim is on the way over to get them back. Without bothering to wash the fruit, I finish it off in a few mouthfuls.

It tastes just as bad as you would imagine: I feel like throwing up. That taste is probably the stench of the mother monkey's mouth. I look up at the branches and toss up some stones. But I fail to knock down a single fruit.

Maybe the fruit was gross to begin with, I think, to comfort myself and get myself to give up on a lost cause that will only bring me grief. But gross is better than not eating at all, and maybe it is just the monkey. I decide to give it a try. I climb up some of the way and see the fruit is still high above me, while below me a mission of monkeys has the tree surrounded.

The mother monkey snitched on me!

The ringleader stands forward, displaying his hairy white chest. The other males follow, screaming together to try to intimidate me.

Maybe this tree is in their turf? Or maybe the mother wants to save face? I wrap my arms around the trunk, not daring to move, but I am practically out of strength.

The monkeys grow impatient.

The leader is the first one up. He catches me and gives me a hard pull. I drop down to the ground and, on rubbery legs, run for dear life.

Looking back, I see the monkeys still at the tree. They have no intention of chasing me. They are embracing in celebration of their victory over an intruder. I stop and catch my breath. Provocatively, the mother is nestling close to the alpha male by her side. He has prised apart her jaws and is scooping out the fruit from her mouth into his own.

I try looking for food further away, but the longer I search the harder it is to push myself. I can no longer think of a reason to keep going. Why not just go home? I use my remaining strength to drag myself to the front door.

Father looks so much older. He actually doesn't tell me off. He just seems very happy to see me. He goes to the kitchen to make me something nice to eat. As I wolf dinner down he takes a feather duster and, sighing, lightly brushes the bear pelt hanging on the wall.

"You know why I don't sell this pelt?" he asks.

"Because… the pelt is the mantle of the Celestial Spirit?"

Is Father trying to make up with me? Will he accept my beloved Bear as a family member as well? Momo must know about the Celestial Spirit. Even if I've never mentioned it to him, he is Grandpa's son. And even though Father killed a bear when he was working in the sawmill, he did it because he had to. Grandpa has surely forgiven him.

"What did you say?"

"The pelt is the mantle of the Celestial Spirit," I say, even more sure of my answer.

Momo laughs, a pained expression on his face. "The Celestial Spirit is one of the figures in the storybook I bought you, isn't it? It's just a story! You took it for real?"

Father pats the back of my neck and tells me not to stuff myself. His palm is unusually cool. He says, "After I killed the bear that year, I discovered that she was carrying twins. I felt so sorry, but feeling sorry wouldn't change anything. Something didn't feel right, though, like retribution or bad luck was just around the corner. I sold her meat but dared not sell her pelt. Later something really did happen to me. My leg got hurt and I couldn't go out and work. Then your mother took sick and died. When she passed away, there was an unborn child in her womb. And now there's a monster out there, neither bear nor ghost, who wants to take away my only son."

He is talking about Kody.

I look up at Father. I want to tell him Kody is not a monster, but I don't open my mouth, because I don't want to upset Father. He looks really gaunt.

13
How to Be a Bear

My days return to normal: school, breadmen, Father and Lotus. I have one less Kody in my life, but one more Bear.

And speaking of bears, Bear isn't the only bear in the mountain forest.

One day around summer solstice, Bear meets another bear. She lowers her head to protect her chin, curls her lips, shows her teeth and snarls. The other bear doesn't want a standoff; he—yes, it's a he-bear—keeps cocking his head to one side, like he is trying to get on Bear's good side. But Bear doesn't appreciate the attention, and soon the new bear leaves.

But when new bear comes round a few days later, things happen rather differently.

The he-bear is even bigger than Bear. This time the he-bear and the she-bear start pushing and shoving, until they fall together on the grass. They are biting each other as they roll around, but they aren't really fighting: it is play-biting and play-fighting.

Because of this he-bear, I see even less of Bear. I only get to watch them from far off.

I imagine Bear hasn't told her boyfriend about me. If she had, the boyfriend wouldn't keep waving his claws at me. Luckily I am fast enough to keep out of his reach.

The time of the temple fair soon comes round again. Father's table of offerings is still popular. This time I get a glutinous carp, while Lotus gets a little wheaten turtle. She lifts it high in the air and places it on her bathroom windowsill. Some passer-by sees it and says Lotus is getting so silly she could be a professional fool.

I am curious. "Why put the turtle on the windowsill? You're not scared someone will take it?"

Lotus has something to give for a change. But I am surprised she is thinking of giving such a nice thing away. I can't help feeling I've underestimated her. But putting it on her windowsill is ridiculous. "Who are you saving it for?"

"I don't know."

"You don't know who to give it to?"

Aside from me, Lotus doesn't have any other friends. Who else can she give it to? Maybe she wants to bribe someone into being her friend and dares not tell me. But she's never lied before, and it doesn't seem like she is lying now.

"Mmmmmmmm…" says Lotus with a vague expression,

as if she really has no idea.

What a joke! "So anyone at all could take it?"

"No!"

Lotus's tone is firm for once. I see she is seriously planning to give it to someone. But there isn't anyone, is there? I tell her, why not just give it to me?

"No way!" Lotus says immediately. "I feel like I'm keeping it for a certain someone I haven't met. Or maybe for a certain someone I have only met once."

I ask her what she means. She dithers for a second, then says, "The person I haven't met is the one who keeps putting things on the windowsill for me."

I keep cross-examining her and find out that this someone has given her lots of things: sometimes a mountain peach, berries or jujubes, and one time half a golden melon.

Lotus scratches her head and says, "At first things got taken from the windowsill. I put the fairy peach there and soon someone took it."

"Oh, so it was you who took the fairy peach!" Afraid I'm going to scold her, Lotus nods meekly.

"That was my peach! You should have given it back to me."

"I didn't know this would happen. I just put it on the windowsill. I didn't take it: someone else did." She looks wounded, but to me this seems like she's being devious. Lotus dishonest? This is a first.

I try to get her to sort out the whole story. "You took it first, right, from my windowsill? You put it on your windowsill and then someone took it. But later on someone started leaving you things on your windowsill, right?"

Lotus thinks for a moment and says, "Yeah."

I have a moment of glee: Kody isn't gone. Apparently he's been watching Lotus's bathroom window to see if there are any "offerings" on the windowsill. And he's been leaving "offerings" for Lotus in return. As for who the certain someone Lotus has met only once is, she doesn't say, and I don't want to know.

I decide to ask Lotus for help. That day I wrap everything up and take her to the Enchanted Thicket. I make her stand under the bat tree holding the whole wheaten carp from the fair in her arms. Even though Kody isn't taking the breadmen from the hollow any more, I hold out hope that he will accept this gift.

One day passes, then another.

By the fourth day, Kody still hasn't appeared. I despair of seeing him and simply give the carp to Lotus.

I go again to the Enchanted Thicket several days later, planning to replace the breadmen in the hollow. I know this is pointless as Kody isn't willing to come and get them. But I still hold out hope that Kody will remember our unspoken pact, or at least that Grandpa will accept it as an offering to him. But this time I find that things aren't as bad as I'd thought. The breadmen from last time are gone! Excitedly, I put new ones in, and when I check again after a couple of days, these are gone too. I go down to ask Lotus, who says she put the carp on her windowsill and that it was gone the very same day along with the wheaten turtle from the fair. I still don't get it: Kody must know who the present on the windowsill is from. Can't he smell my scent on it? If so, Father's scent is also on the offering too. Kody should be able to smell that as well. Father tried to kill him. Wouldn't Kody be afraid?

Maybe he really isn't scared any more and that's why he is taking the breadmen again. He even leaves a bunch of berries in the bat tree hollow to thank me.

Still, he isn't willing to show himself. I search the hills but can't find him... until one day, I see a black form hiding among the rocks.

Kody is covered head to paw in claw and bite marks. Still, he is bigger now, and now there is a definite glint of gloomy majesty in his eyes, cold and fierce.

Over time we become as close as we've ever been. I take him to the Cataract Cave, behind the curtain of the waterfall, to see the latest acquisitions in the Treasure Troves. I also teach him to recognize the eggs of every bird, of yellow chickadees, white-tail robins, yellow-belly bush warblers, Formosan laughingthrushes, green-wing doves, grey-cheek thrushes, green woodpeckers, yellow-belly prinias...

Kody doesn't understand these names, but he can't help being interested in these treasures. He strokes the eggs with approval in his eyes like a true connoisseur. But his hand-paws aren't as nimble as regular hands are, and he accidentally drops one.

I rush to inspect the pieces of cracked egg. They are a light pastel shade with red speckles.

"This one's a red chickadee's egg!"

I only have this one red chickadee's egg, and it was tough to find. But now that Kody is with me it doesn't matter if all the eggs get cracked. I continue to guide him round the layout of the cave. I take him through the labyrinth to see the stalactites. And I let him sleep in the cradle. There isn't space in that stone cradle for a fully grown bear, but there is just enough space for Kody and me.

This is the ideal den. It has everything one could need. There is food in the Treasure Troves and spring water in the sinks. On the other side of the waterfall is a pool of fish and shrimp. Every day at noon when I get out from school I can't wait to come up here to the Cataract Cave and see Kody. I take coloured pencils, paper and the storybook Father bought for me, so I can colour and caption Kody's story.

"Look, this is you writing words from inside the cage. This is you in the Enchanted Thicket. You're eating the breadmen from the bat tree hollow.

"Later you make friends with Lotus. You take the fairy peach from her windowsill."

Kody listens as I colour and tell his story. He says "oh" a couple of times, as if he understands.

I teach him to recognize some other words and, holding his paw in my hand, to write out some more words on the ground, letter by letter: "big", "little", "you" and "me"…

But no matter how I teach him or how many times we practise, Kody still isn't sure what words are, nor is he willing to write. When he grips the pencil he just groans. Maybe I shouldn't be so intent on teaching him.

Bears don't need to write, after all. Then again, Kody isn't a bear.

But if he isn't a bear, what is he? No matter what, he

can't be a monster.

No, Kody isn't a monster. He is only a boy who thinks he is a bear, that's all. When he sees the resemblance between the bear in the book and himself, he has a moment of self-recognition. But Kody doesn't know how to be a bear. All he knows is trying to model himself on the pictures in the storybook, and the best he can manage is a crude imitation of an imitation: the pictures aren't real bears, either.

All I can do is teach Kody everything I know about being a bear, all the bear calls and gestures, all the bear lore I can remember.

At first, when Kody climbs up a tree like one of the bears in the book, he falls right back down.

He tries to pluck honey, but the second he touches the hive he is besieged by bees.

Kody tries to build a nest by copying a bear in the storybook, but it ends up looking like a pile of trash.

Later Kody finally learns to hunt, pluck honey, claw bark, build a nest, just like a real bear. He thrusts out his throat, flattens his ears, bares his teeth, curls his lips and says *Awwwwwwooooo* and *Grrrrrrrrr* like a bear. But Kody just isn't a bear. His sound isn't quite right. His ears don't stand up like a bear's. And when he calls it is just an *Ooooo* or a *Huuummmm*, which is usually answered by a chorus of wild dogs.

What is Kody?

I often grasp Kody's paw and help him draw pictures in my book of bears.

First we draw a boy and I point at myself. Then I get him to try to draw himself.

But Kody can only scribble. It is all stiff lines and strange curves.

I keep on teaching him, and finally he is able to draw a simple silhouette, neither bear nor boy.

One time, I draw a human father and mother holding a baby, indicating that this is a picture of me and my parents. Then I motion for him to draw himself and his parents. But Kody just stands there.

"You don't know your father and mother?"

Kody looks baffled.

Another time, I draw a cabin in the woods and let Kody know this is a picture of my home. But when it is his turn to draw, he doesn't do anything.

"You don't know where your home is?"

Again, bafflement.

Then one time I draw the martial arts performer-cum-tonic hawker and Kody in his cage.

"This is you, Kody. And this is the tonic hawker."

This gets a reaction out of him: he immediately starts whining.

"What is the connection between you and the hawker?"

Kody draws for me, but it is more of the same, illegible squiggles and hooks.

I know I have to keep the questions simple or he won't understand. I struggle for the right words and the right way. With pictures and hints, I gradually guide his drawing, asking him questions every step of the way.

Slowly the story begins unfolding in pictures. When Kody needs more space, I stick in some more sheets of paper at the end of the storybook. I do this again and again—sometimes it works, sometimes it doesn't. Several months later the children's storybook has become like an album, so thick it is bursting at the seams. Kody's story has a beginning and a middle, though not yet an end.

I see the tonic hawker taking a little boy home.

The hawker has a real bear, but later on it gets sick and dies.

After the bear dies, the hawker puts it in an icy vault and flays its skin off strip by strip.

The salesman pokes and pricks the boy's skin until it is red and inflamed. Onto the boy's skin he sprinkles some kind of medicinal powder. Then he attaches the patches of bear pelt to the boy.

The boy is "Kody".

The hawker makes Kody take medicine that burns his throat. Kody will never talk again.

The hawker cuts Kody's fingers short, turning his hands into paws…

The hawker teaches Kody to perform. When he wields the whip, Kody writes.

The hawker teaches Kody to jump through a ring of fire. When Kody won't jump, the hawker beats him.

Kody howls, and dogs gather outside his house… Kody escapes his chains. When the hawker catches Kody, the dogs surround and attack him, letting Kody escape.

I look at Kody, his pelt a patchy mess, with tears in my eyes. "Kody, promise me you'll stay in the Cataract Cave, all right? I'll make things for you to eat. Don't go out there again. There's too many bad people in the world."

Kody shifts around, like he doesn't want to listen.

"Kody, you listen to me. It's too dangerous. You can't leave this cave, let alone this mountain."

But Kody won't listen.

When he leaves, the leaves are falling like rain on the other side of the waterfall.

14
Word Gets Out

Kody doesn't winter in Cataract Cave. Though he regularly returns to take breadmen from the Enchanted Thicket, he ranges further and comes back with more and more scars. As for Bear, she returns in spring, with two little ones by her side.

Bear is now a mother bear. She doesn't try to avoid me, but now she only lets me watch from a distance as she trains her cubs to catch fish, pluck fruit, poke anthills and steal hives.

The cubs are just as smart as their mother. They know how to dislodge a hive from a tree into the water to drown the bees and scoop out the honey. My disciple Kody isn't as adept as the cubs and often gets bitten into a panic without getting a single mouthful of honey.

One time Kody stumbles upon a hornet's nest. He runs

away like lightning, but still gets stung a few times. The stings well up and there is soon a bloody purple discharge. I remember something the beekeeper told me and I only half-believed. I hurriedly gather spiders.

When I set the first black spider on one of Kody's stings it clamps down on it. Slowly its stomach begins expanding. I almost can't bear to watch. Watching that spider sucking so savagely, I start to regret my attempted cure and worry that I won't be able to get it off without it taking a chunk out of Kody.

But a while later, the spider falls off on its own, dead.

I inspect Kody's wound. It is much better, just as the beekeeper said. Black spiders will suck out the venom from a wound for you until they are poisoned to death.

But I'm not sure why black spiders do this. Don't they know it's fatal? Maybe it's natural greed or bloodlust. As long as there is blood they will suck, unable to tell if the blood contains poison.

As for the bees that bit Kody, they were no longer young. Maybe they were even elderly. As the beekeeper told me, three days after finally pupating, bees start working in the hexagonal cells inside the hive, making beeswax, collecting pollen, secreting royal jelly and serving the queen and drones. Sixteen days later these worker bees are already old, only able to go in search of honey plants or to guard the home fort. It seems to me that these bees that stung Kody were defending the nest even though they were about to die. I stay on the lookout for dead bees on the trail and in the woods, but as before I don't find a single one.

Maybe these warriors have already taken refuge in the abode of the great Celestial Bee and have flown to a mountain higher. When I tell Grandpa, I hear him laugh. Kody is trying hard to learn to be a bear, but he just can't do it. He seems more like a monkey. Once I find him sitting up in a tree grooming a squirrel just like a monkey would. Another time I see him hanging from a branch, scooping fish from a stream.

He doesn't attack his prey like a bear, nor is he as ferocious and powerful as a bear. He is pretty skilled, though, at climbing vines, leaping and swinging, scaling rocks and plucking fruit. But he is more skilled at stealing food than in getting it by force.

He only has one reason to be proud of himself. When he comes out of the water and shakes off the water, from a distance he actually does resemble a bear. But that's all: he can shake his fur a bit like a bear but he can't swim, only paddle around the shallows. Still, he thinks he can swim. Every time I see Kody swimming merrily into deep water, I have to tear off my trousers, tie off the ends to trap the air inside, and throw them to him as a life preserver.

There are now so many chicks that Lotus has no time to give them all names. So she just calls them all "Precious".

Though the name makes me think Lotus treasures the chicks, she no longer works as hard caring for them. She is often late for work or goes home early. One of Father's breadmen isn't a special treat for her any more. Maybe she's even got a bit tired of them. She is a decent person, so she still keeps coming to the house, but now working in the coop is a chore or a duty, not a passion. Father feels uneasy. He worries the chicks aren't being properly cared for and orders me not to run off after school.

Because of this, I make a special trip to the Enchanted Thicket to ask for a leave of absence. "Grandpa, I have to go home earlier now. Momo's afraid the chicks will run off. If that happens he'll get angry."

Grandpa expresses no opinion about this. Just when I am leaving, though, several crows caw. It makes my heart thump. On the trunks of the trees where the crows are roosting, there are several long tracks of climbing ants. I follow them up with my eyes and am surprised to see a number of ant nests. My heartbeat feels heavy: I remember a prophecy in a dream in which Grandpa said, *When you see lots of ant nests in the trees, be wary of mountain torrents after rain.*

I tell Father, "Be careful. It might start pouring today."

"But it's so hot. We could use a nice deluge."

So I say, "Maybe the stream will flood."

"We'll be safe. I should probably get you another book, maybe without pictures this time. You carry the old one around so much it's a wonder you don't disappear into it."

He doesn't get me a new book. It doesn't rain. I wait a couple of days, and finally my worry fades, and my disappointment too. Now I only care about one thing, though it isn't anything important. At the most it is a source of bafflement.

Snakes. I've never been much concerned with them before.

The snake I spot slides away as soon as it sees me. I check to make sure all the chicks are still in the coop and tell Father when he gets home. Father says snakes are a part of living in the mountains. He scatters lime powder around the house and the coop and tells me not to be afraid. "Mountain kids shouldn't be afraid of snakes, especially boys."

I ask Lotus, "Are you scared of snakes?"

"Nope."

"You got bitten and you're still not scared!"

"It doesn't hurt any more. What's there to be afraid of?"

Lotus has seen snakes before in the coop. She just trilled at them. They were gone in a flash.

"With the lime around the house, how are they getting in?" I am baffled.

Lotus doesn't see the problem. "Snakes climb trees. If they can't go on the ground they'll just go by branch, or over the roof. If they have no other way, they can fly through the air..."

For once Lotus knows something I don't know. "How do you know snakes can wriggle on the roof or even fly?"

"I've seen a snake fly."

I don't believe her, but Lotus isn't a liar. Maybe she imagined it. I tell Lotus to come a bit earlier, and that she mustn't slack off or we'll lose all the chicks.

This time I manage to get through to her. She starts coming on time. I supervise her a couple of times and she is working really hard. Now I can go out to play!

I notice changes in the forest. Mother Bear and her two cubs have staked out a territory. The three of them have left claw marks and piss on all the trunks and stumps in the area. They seem to have settled in.

I go round the vicinity and discover a beast spring, which any bear can find on instinct. Grandpa told me this kind of spring will never go dry no matter how serious the drought. It seems Mother Bear has found a good one, with plenty of fruit and prey—the creatures that come to drink at the spring.

But word gets out. One day there is an intruder, a huge he-bear, but not the same he-bear as before. He chases the cubs, who whine in panic and scurry over to Mother Bear's side. I can't get away, so I jump into a den beside me, pulling old vines over to cover the entryway.

I see Mother Bear signalling towards a mountain wall. One of the cubs gets the message, charges to the foot of the wall and climbs right up.

The other cub freezes. Mother Bear pats his behind, and finally he wakes up, whines, and half-rolls, half-runs to the foot of the wall. Then he climbs on up. When he gets to the top he sits beside his brother, looking down through a clump of grass.

Mother Bear looks up as if to tell them, or herself, not to worry. Then she turns to meet the he-bear.

Their fur stands on end. They roar at each other. And then they spring.

The male gives the female a whack on the head. Furious, the female strikes back with a paw to the belly.

The male knocks her off balance and sends her tumbling to the ground.

But as she is falling she swipes at his leg. He tumbles

too. They turn into a rolling, biting, howling furball. Their teeth gnash. They suck the air and kick up dust. Tufts of hair go flying.

The he-bear has a weight advantage, and though Mother Bear growls more fiercely, she is just flailing at him, hitting nothing but air. Their front paws dangle over the edge of the rock wall, and the cubs yelp in earnest. But they don't sound anxious or upset. It is like they are cheering on prize fighters.

Their mother, below, is now seriously wounded. She tries to crawl away but is dragged back by the male.

She is too tired to fight back. She just holds her head and tries to avoid his strikes. There is blood in his eyes. Every blow is ruthless, every strike potentially deadly.

I see Mother Bear in grave danger and worry that the male will turn to me and the cubs after finishing her off. The ants in the den are biting me to death, but I have no time to smack them off. Ants! Suddenly I remember the willow whistle in my pocket. I get it out and start to play as loudly as I can, changing tunes and tempos to get the effect I want.

The bears are still rolling on the ground, but now they are throwing fewer strikes.

Soon they stop completely. Each one rolls into a ball and starts scratching.

Mother Bear seems to understand what I am trying to tell her. She rolls further and further away. This is her only chance.

Once she has gone a certain distance I stop playing. The he-bear stands up, unsteady. By this time Mother Bear has already hid herself up a tree. The male gazes lazily up at the canopy, shilly-shallies over to the spring to wash and rinse out his mouth. He grooms himself very carefully, and slowly gives all his wounds soothing licks. It seems that the battle hasn't been worth it. All he's got out of it is a crumpled coat.

The male sits by the spring, still panting. Finally, after resting a while longer, he slowly starts walking away.

He's probably just been planning to have a drink, not occupy the territory. Maybe he's decided that capturing the spring was too much work for too little gain. Or perhaps he is afraid of the mysterious power of my whistle.

Finally he is gone. Mother Bear slowly comes down, looks up at the mountain wall and signals. Her cubs rush down and snuggle by her side. They are crying and crooning. It doesn't sound like they are mourning their mother's injuries so much as trying to get attention.

She is badly wounded. She licks herself a bit but is mostly concerned with checking the squirming cubs for harm. Finding none, she swiftly pats their fur smooth and washes their faces to make them presentable again, before finally letting them go and play.

I am worried about Mother Bear. But if I am late I'll get into trouble with Father. I make it home at dusk.

The next day I find they've already moved to a new territory. I search through the woods calling, "Mother Bear! Moooooother Bear!" Silence.

The third day, I find Mother Bear on a path. At her last gasp, she has not been able to answer my calls. The cubs' calls have led me to her.

I think of treating her wounds, but it would be hard to find those balms the herbalist taught me. Luckily the ones I collected with him are still in the Forbidden Room. They'll come in handy at last. I rush home and carry the medicine back to where Mother Bear is lying. I try to remember the preparations he taught me: some herbs you pound, other you smoke, still others you juice. Once I finish applying the medicines, her wounds start to show improvement, but her body is still weak.

Whenever she has the strength to go on, Mother Bear finds a new place for herself and the cubs. I exhaust myself keeping track of them, until, one day, Mother Bear leaves the cover of the forest and comes near the Forbidden Room. She is probably attracted by the smell of medicine, which she associates with the healing of her wounds. But it might also be Grandpa's influence leading her here. Whatever the reason, she shouldn't have come. I shoo her away, but how can I be sure she won't come back?

15
Out of Bounds

I am later than normal. But I should have been all right. Father rarely comes home this early.

"Don't you get off school at noon today? Where have you been all afternoon?" Father sits at the table clipping his fingernails, like he is waiting for the truth. I say I went to a classmate's house. He looks up at me. "No you didn't. You went climbing. Lotus told me everything." All I can do is admit it and promise not to come home late again.

Father doesn't look pleased. He speaks very slowly, as if he doesn't want to threaten me for fear I'll leave home again. "It's not that I don't want to let you go, it's that I'm afraid you're too small and you'll get into trouble. Please don't lie to me." I say I won't. He sweeps up the fingernail clippings on the floor. "You can go exploring, but don't come home so late." He walks to the stove and gets ready to bake. As for Lotus the secret sharer, she just sits there on my stool eating breadmen, not even looking at me. Father notices the bits of sugar on her lips, brushes them off and tells her to go home.

Later I ask Lotus, "Why did you tell on me?"

She swallows and says, "Your father asked me, so I told him."

There is nothing wrong with that. I never asked Lotus to lie for me, and even if I had she wouldn't have been able to do it. But for the sake of Mother Bear and the cubs I think I should keep my distance from Lotus so she won't keep leaking information.

But then one day Lotus just doesn't show up! Maybe because I've not been smiling at her enough lately? I never meant for her to feel like I blame her!

The very first evening, her family comes over. Father says he doesn't know where Lotus has gone.

Lotus doesn't come back the second day, either. Father is beside himself. He goes out looking for her instead of setting up his stand.

Another few days and still no Lotus. And no Father, either. I spend the nights alone, my eyes wide open, watching the bats flap around in the shadows. I don't get a wink of sleep.

Another two days pass before Father finally comes

back. His face looks terrible, and on his hand there is an inflamed wound.

"I've taken Lotus home to her parents," said Father.

"Where'd she go all this time?"

"Lotus was with a snake charmer. I had a talk with the young fellow and he didn't abduct her or anything. It was Lotus who kept begging to go with him. I started pulling on Lotus's arm, and she began yelling. Then the charmer's snake shot out and bit me..."

Seeing Father had been bitten because of her, Lotus no longer resisted and obediently followed him home. But she doesn't want to stay where she isn't wanted, so she comes to our house as usual to watch over our chickens.

I ask her, "You really wanted to go with that snake charmer?"

Lotus seems not to be able to explain herself, except by saying that the snakes listened to her and she wanted to play with them.

"How could those snakes understand you?"

"That snake charmer told the snakes not to bite me, so they didn't. He told them to play with me, so they played with me."

I finally understand why she was coming late and leaving early all that time. She was playing with the snakes. And the "certain someone she had met only once" to whom she wanted to give a gift of gratitude must have been the snake charmer.

I ask Lotus to teach me some snake charmer's signals. She says she doesn't know any.

"How does the snake charmer train snakes?" I ask.

"I didn't see."

I keep asking, but Lotus won't say anything, except: "That's a secret."

I never thought Lotus would keep a secret. I am sorry I underestimated her. Maybe I've been wrong to keep her at a distance recently.

Finally I ask, "Did that snake charmer abduct you? Or did you want to go with him?"

Lotus says, "He didn't force me, no. I didn't want to go home."

"Does that mean you'd forgotten about us and your responsibilities here?"

"When the chicks are ready for market you'll just slaughter them." Lotus looks sad, as if she's finally realized why every so often the coop has been short of a bunch of chickens.

"You don't want to eat my father's breadmen, either?"

Lotus says she doesn't mind them, but her expression seems to say: "They're good, but I'm getting sick of them." I ask her more about the snake charmer. She won't or can't give me any details. She makes him out to be a regular person, just one who gets snake bites and knows about antidotes. But finally there is a question she is able to answer clearly.

"He's a nice person." She has the same expression as when she talks about Father.

I want to make it up with Lotus. She is willing, but she doesn't seem as happy as before. So I ask her, "Are you still thinking about snakes?"

Lotus says, "I stole two chicks to feed the snakes without

letting your father know."

"I'll keep it confidential. Chickens lay like crazy, and Momo doesn't keep an inventory. Don't worry, he won't find out."

Lotus breathes a sigh of relief and agrees to be my friend again. Now she is even more careful about looking after the chicks. As a hen gathers chicks under her wings, so Lotus crouches in the coop and gathers the chicks under her apron, trying to keep her skirts on the ground. Probably feeling guilty about Lotus doing so much extra work for free, Father is nicer and nicer to her. He gives her my stool to sit on, and steams an extra banana cake for her every evening. Those are supposed to be for me! If the breadmen don't sell out, he gives Lotus first choice.

With Lotus on duty, I can go off on my own. I make her promise not to tell Father under any circumstances. She promises, and her face makes me feel there isn't anyone in the whole world you can count on more than her.

Certainly she can't count on me. Because I ate some of her chicks.

Father took a basket of eggs that were ready to hatch and put them in the steamer. He even told Lotus to put wood in the stove.

From inside the steamer we heard the cheeps of unhatched chicks, delicate and sweet. They didn't sound like death cries.

They would have hatched in a day or two—some of them had already started trying to poke through. Father said, "These are called blood eggs. They're good for you."

"Why steam so many all at once?"

"If you don't eat them before they hatch, then they're not blood eggs."

Blood eggs have a distinctive smell, strong and raw, but they are still very edible. When I offer a few to Lotus, she starts crying and won't answer.

Later on, Lotus admits to taking an egg.

She looks like she is afraid I'll get angry or ask for it back. Only when I promise I won't bother over a single egg does she say, "I put it on my belly button when I'm sleeping, then cover it with the blanket. In a couple of days it's gonna hatch."

Hatch it does. She calls the chick Chanticleer and takes it everywhere with her. It eats and plays in the pocket of her apron. In less than two months, the infant peeps become loud cock-a-doodle-doos. Less than one month after that, Lotus's family goes and makes soup out of Lotus's rooster.

Lotus keeps coming to look after the chickens like nothing has happened, only now she cock-a-doodle-doos faintly at them instead of cheeping or peeping. She must be in mourning.

I tell her that the next time we steam blood eggs, I'll let her keep back one of the eggs to incubate.

She says she won't want to hatch it. I say I won't want to eat them.

Father seems to know about our agreement and stops telling Lotus to steam blood eggs or me to eat them. But then I am getting stronger, so maybe Father feels I don't need to eat them any more.

One day, Lotus takes me to see Chanticleer's grave, saying, "It's Chanticleer's protection that's stopped your father from steaming blood eggs."

I ask her, "How do you know the eggs are under Chanticleer's protection?"

"Chanticleer's become the Celestial Chicken. He protects all chickens, fair or foul, that they may hatch and grow up and not be eaten."

Lotus is dead serious. She leads me towards the grave and we pay our respects to the dead. The grave is impressive: she says all the chicken bones are buried in the mound. And she erected a wooden tablet for Chanticleer.

"You say Chanticleer's become a spirit?" I think about the unusual note in Lotus's voice.

"Chanticleer told me." Lotus dreamed of Chanticleer with a pouch slung over his shoulder, a curved knife hung at his waist, his body luminous.

I pass what Lotus said to Grandpa, telling him chickens have a Celestial Spirit too. Would the Celestial Bear eat the Celestial Chicken when it got hungry? I know Grandpa won't eat Lotus's beloved Chanticleer—he's just the Guardian of the Celestial Spirit—but I want him to pass the message on to the Celestial Spirit—the Big Bear in the sky—Himself.

In addition to looking after the chickens in the coop, Lotus sometimes waits on Father. But now she does more than swat away flies and mosquitoes. One time I peep through a hole in the roof-tiles and see her doing unto Father as the she-monkeys did unto the alpha male. Her hands are at his belly, then lower, not like she is lousing him, however. She just cups his willy with her hands and squeezes softly. When she finally relaxes her fingers, they spread out like the petals of a sacred lotus flower; and at the centre of the flower, standing straight up, is an enchanted snake, which slowly softens, settles back into the base of her palms and is gone.

For a while I try to be good, taking care to be home before dark every day. But it doesn't seem to matter. Father doesn't seem to mind no matter how late I am, and no matter how late I stay out Lotus is there when I get home. But she isn't looking after the chicks. I counted. We were two short. Father laughs and says it is nothing. He let Lotus take them home.

One day I choose the wrong day to come home late. I go to check on the chickens as usual. But before I reach the coop a shadow holding two hens rushes out. I break out in a cold sweat and run into the house. It was a bear. I am sure it was an adult bear. I saw two green lights like glowworms, and not for the first time.

The situation in the house is scarier still. Father and Kody are brawling.

Father grabs an axe and starts chasing Kody.

As Kody runs, he throws things to try to block the way.

Lotus is hiding under the bed, crying. There is a bloody bite mark on Father's arm.

Suddenly, Kody throws my stool at Father and the head of the axe gets knocked off, leaving Father holding the handle. I run to pick up the axe-head to throw at Kody, as Kody runs at Father.

When the axe-head hits Kody, he lets go of Father and flees. When he reaches the door, he turns and looks. It is a look of hatred, the look of an enemy who was once a friend.

I begin sobbing, as if to say: He's my father! I had no other choice!

But Father refuses to leave it at that. There is a terrible rage in his eyes. He grabs a torch and tears out into the night. Soon I hear a hubbub outside.

I look out and there is a line of torches and barking hounds cutting through the alpine forest.

I yank down the pelt on the wall for protection and charge out.

Everyone is looking for Kody. I am too. By intuition I take a shortcut—I know I'll find him in the Cataract Cave.

There, I hear a soft whining sound.

Kody! Kody! I call to him as I feel around in the dark. There are some glowworms on the wall of the cave. I rip a strip from my shirt and wrap them inside to make a wormlamp.

"I knew you'd be here." In the faint light, Kody is huddled inside the cradle, trembling as he licks his bloody wound. When he sees me he begins weeping.

He's badly wounded. "Kody, I'm sorry!" I say.

He lets me sit beside him and even licks me. I pat him, saying, "I know, I know, you forgive me."

I look in alarm at the blood oozing from Kody's wound. I pray for a miracle, but then I remember something practical.

I look around.

I am looking for the web of a certain kind of spider. I know it by pattern and colour. The herbalist said if I ever cut myself by accident, all I'd need to do to stop the blood and the burn is find this kind of web. Even though Kody's cut is deep, the web should still have some effect.

I look in every nook and cranny and finally gather enough webs. I peel off the rough outer sheet of each web and use the flexible inner core to wrap up Kody's wound, layer by layer. But every layer gets soaked with blood. I don't know why it's not working. I look helplessly at Kody.

He looks back at me with gratitude.

I tell him, "Grandpa will protect you," knowing very well that Grandpa isn't there.

Kody drags himself along, reaching out with his paw and dipping it in the water in one of the sinks on the bed of the cave.

I bring the wormlamp near. He starts painting on the wall. Somehow I understand the story he is trying to tell:

Father is pressed on Lotus's body—they are like two bears rolling around in the bushes.

Lotus's hands are hugging Father. Father's mouth is open as if to bite her.

Watching from outside the window, Kody rushes in and bites Father.

Father lets Lotus go and starts chasing Kody.

There are dogs and men outside the cave. I know the lynch mob has arrived, perhaps following the drops of blood to the entrance of the cave. The waterfall cannot hide us, for in the drought of winter the screen of water is too thin.

From the outside they can easily see in.

Torches encircle the pond. Someone holds a torch near and shouts, "Look! There's something inside!"

They begin wading over, throwing their brands into the cave, which soon becomes thick with smoke.

I drag Kody into the labyrinth. Beyond is the stalactite chamber, but I don't know if the rear exit is open or not. It depends whether we can dislodge the swallow's nests from the hollows in Swallow's Cliff soon enough.

The firelight is nearer now. I decide to let Kody go on ahead and try to draw off the pursuit myself. I need to create a diversion. I drape the bear pelt over my head and charge towards the edge of the cave.

"There it is!" someone says, right before I leap into the crowded pool. The clubs of the search party raise to strike.

"There it is!" There is a great howl. Everyone stops moving.

The voice says again, "Look at that huge bear! Over there! Let's get it!" All the torchlight and barking starts moving in the direction the man who spoke is pointing. In the confusion someone pulls me up out of the water, lifts up the sodden bearskin I'm wearing and slaps me. I see Father glaring at me. But before he has the chance to tell me off we are swept along with the others, along the mountain slope.

Finally, we can see the Enchanted Thicket by torchlight, with Swallow's Cliff above and Devil's Gulch below. A bellowing shadow stands among the trees of the elfinwood. It's the shadow of a bear.

The gang charges. Bear turns and runs.

The fastest runners in the mob have almost caught up with Bear, but Bear can run faster than any man. She is sprinting now, moving as fast as a celestial being. Suddenly she leaps across the emptiness onto a thin, silvery beam of light that leads the way like a razor's edge out of Devil's Gulch up past Swallow's Cliff into the sky—but at that very instant a black cloud billows out of Devil's Gulch. Before you know it, millions of bats obscure the sky.

At least one thing was certain. We stopped losing chickens.

Someone said he saw a pile of chicken bones and feathers in a bear's nest somewhere. He thought they must be from our chickens. But nobody managed to catch any bears, or any cubs. And I never personally saw the nest.

Not long after, Father said it was time for us to move. He sold the chickens and the bear pelt and said we were leaving and never coming back. We moved so far that for the longest time I couldn't find the way home.

More than once in my new life I dreamed about the cabin in the clearing in the woods. In the dreams the cabin is dilapidated: the doorway is covered in cobwebs, the yard overgrown with weeds, the bamboo palisade has collapsed and the coop is empty—though for some reason I can hear chickens calling, just like the day we left. Father was packing up and I kept hearing chickens call, even though we'd already sold them all.

On the day of the move, I asked Father where we were moving to, but he refused to tell me. Instead, in a tone of voice he'd usually reserved for storytelling, he said, "Our new house is made of cement. It's stronger and more comfortable than this one. It even has glass windows!"

"Will Grandpa move too?"

"Grandpa's dead. He doesn't have to move."

Father had often heard me mention Grandpa. That was the first time he told me directly that Grandpa was dead.

"I've got to tell Grandpa we're moving," I said. Father asked me where I was going. "To the Enchanted Thicket." I told him about the shoulder-like outcrop that overlooks Devil's Gulch.

Father said Grandpa wasn't there. I insisted he was and that he could hear me when I spoke to him. Father only repeated, weakly, "He's not there." I asked him where he was. Father said he didn't know, that nobody knew. "He died during an air raid. We never found his body."

"But he is there." I was adamant.

Father looked weary and bothered. "He is not."

No matter what, I believed he was there. I thought, why else would Cub—or Bear—draw away the pursuit like that to save Kody? I was sure she'd been summoned by Grandpa, the Guardian of the Celestial Spirit, or maybe Bear was one of Grandpa's incarnations. I didn't say any of this to Father, because he said that Bear had fallen into Devil's Gulch and was probably dead. I said, "Bear's spirit would have followed the moonlight past the highest peak."

Father said, "That's just a picture in the storybook I bought you."

"That book tells the story of our tribe."

"And what tribe is that?"

I couldn't say. Grandpa had never told me, and I'd never asked.

Father hoisted our luggage on his back and took my hand. In front of the gate, he quietly said, "Maybe once upon a time we were hunters in these hills. But now we don't belong to any tribe. We adopted Chinese ways a long time ago."

It's been so long since I left that I don't remember the name of the village any more.

Momo never mentioned the name, but I've found the village after much searching. I'm finally home.

The thing is, everywhere I go I feel vaguely uneasy. It's an uncanny feeling, that something isn't quite right. Swallow's Cliff is pretty steep, but it isn't sheer, the way I remember it. The Enchanted Thicket isn't at all mysterious. Devil's Gulch isn't especially dark.

I crouch by the bat tree with the hollow. Grandpa's gravestone used to be right by this tree. Now there is nothing there.

I try to judge where the urn used to be and start digging. To my surprise, I find it. I put the red shell I've brought inside, seal it and bury it again.

"All twelve shells are here now, Grandpa."

I lower my head, and mumble at where the stone used to be. Nobody can hear what I say, except maybe Grandpa.

Then, from the canopy of the Enchanted Thicket, comes a soft choral melody, rising in crescendo:

i likihli likihli iui i lavahli lavahli
ina muli vengeeli iui mulilalee vuai
ina mataru taruuhl iui matalalee vuai
ina hlisapeta vinau i saramarukaruka
ina vengavenga vihluua i kupatarahlapee
kupatarahlapee kumiakui iaiai

The spleenwort fronds in moonlight clear the fog,
And flames are dancing on a ribwood log.
Our patewood cups are filled with mead and grog,
Beneath the routbaum roasts a feral hog.

Epilogue
Dream Writer

The year I turned twelve Father came back from a solitary summer trip to the mountains. In autumn, he started walking—and writing—in his sleep. I would see him get up in the middle of the night, scribble pictures and captions in an album, then go into the backyard to dig a hole in the ground. One night in the dead of winter, Father got up in the middle of the night and came up to my bed. He stood there with staring eyes, but he wasn't looking at me. He wasn't looking at what was in front of him, either. He seemed a sad spirit, old and weary, not like my father, not even like a living human being. That night, he left and didn't come back. I sat up in bed wrapped in my blanket all night long. I couldn't hear him in the backyard. Shivering, I wondered whether I should go out in pursuit. But I'd never bothered him before. I'd been like an unimportant appendage to his life for twelve years. Dawn came and I never saw Father again.

Curious about what it was he used to get up in the middle of the night to write or draw, I took his keys and opened all his drawers and found that scrapbook he'd started when he was ten. Later I dug up a cabinet he'd buried in the backyard. That cabinet contained a treasure, an album in which Father had recorded his childhood.

But I discovered that the handwriting in the scrapbook and the album he left behind was the same. As a man, Father continued to write in the cramped hand of a boy. And the dates he signed in the album, which he'd written in the autumn of 1988 at the age of thirty-four, were from when he was ten years old to the age of twelve, from 1964 to 1966.

As if he'd never got any older than twelve years old.

As if he'd never left childhood.

By reading his scrapbook and his album I started prying into his childhood secrets. I like to think he wouldn't have minded, that he had memorialized his childhood to keep me company. For Father never spoke, was never able to speak, about his childhood memories. I heard that when he was twelve years old, after Momo took him away from his home in the hills to live in the big city, he suddenly caught a rare virus that left him unable to speak. Henceforth, he could only communicate with his hands.

He could still hear, though. Whenever he heard birdsong, or animal cries, a happy or intent expression would appear upon his face.

I never knew my mother. There was only a woman in a yellowed photograph. I've always thought of her as my mother, but maybe she was my grandmother. That photograph was really old.

I kept Father's story secret as I grew up. I was alone, but never lonely.

One day, I decided to finish the album Father had left behind. I was a bit like a translator, I guess, turning Father's diary-in-pictures into a diary-in-prose. In doing so, I turned Father's story into my own childhood fable. After I grew up, in the summer of 1997, I visited the mountains Father had depicted in his album. There was indeed a temple on a plain near the rise of the foothills, but by then it had long been abandoned. There was no square in front of the temple. I didn't see the ethereal alpine quality captured in Father's illustrations. There weren't polychromatic clouds lingering around the peaks, and the sounds in the woods were from black drongos and jackdaws, not laughingthrushes or chickadees. In the meagre mixed groves of deciduous and evergreen trees, there were no lovely osmanthus or magnolia blooms. And there were no snow plums or camellias growing in the layer of fallen leaves and branches on the ground.

I made my way up a narrow mountain path. The tall tufts of silver grass lining the path almost hid the way ahead, and engulfed my shadow as soon as I passed through. I reached the end of the path and found myself at an abandoned orchard. The rotten fruits scattered on the ground had attracted some garishly bright butterflies and beetles.

I kept walking and came to the overgrown base of a precipitous slope and discovered a disused corduroy road and, running parallel to it, a deserted railway from the Japanese era. On a road up a neighbouring mountain, I came upon a store, the only one in the area. It sold fresh mountain produce, namely snake soup and sautéed spleenwort.

I greeted the proprietress. She said her name was Lotus. And that husband of hers in charge of killing the snakes they sold? He had delicate and beautiful features, like a girl's. I asked him his name as well. He slowly looked up at me and said, gently, "Up here in the mountains, names are unnecessary." Then he returned to tossing strips of freshly killed snake into a barrel.

I looked for signs of naivety or idiocy in Lotus, but her movements were deft, her eyes bright. She simply asked me what I would like to buy. What else was there in the store? She sold me a can of beer and a bag of peanuts. I downed the beer and got a closer look at her when I paid the bill. There was no regret in her face, just a forlorn feeling about her. I wanted to ask her if she knew my father and grandfather, if she was the Lotus illustrated in the pages of my father's album, but I decided there was no point. The old lady sitting beside me on the train was called Lotus. The girl on the path selling straw hats was Lotus as well. The village woman pulling a cart of lumber down the mountain was named Lotus. In Chinese, Lotus is a very common name.

"I met Lotus. Just not your Lotus." So I told Father silently when I left the store. Father, who was hanging in the air like a fog that wouldn't lift, said not a word in reply.

Then from behind me came a clucking sound. It sounded like a hen!

Startled, I looked back. A hen flapped into the store. Lotus scattered a handful of rice on the dirt floor, which the hen began to peck.

I turned to ask her, "Can you make the sound of a chicken?" She blinked at me. "Do you raise hens?"

Lotus said, "No, she's wild. She likes to come into the store and peck around in nooks and crannies. I usually give her something to eat." She finished explaining, and then, as if in response to my first question, started teasing the hen: "*Cluuuuuuck cluck cluck…*"

It actually sounded like the crowing of an old and feeble rooster. I smiled.

But I can't say I felt any disappointment. I knew I would never find the remains of the old village Father had described, for every trace of colour had been wiped away by years of wind and rain.

But I still like to play the following scenes in my imagination, as if I'm editing a montage in my mind's eye:

In February, the muntjac loses its horns.
The leaf beetles and scarabs eat holes in the leaves.
The sticky secretions of aphids and woodlice form plant galls.
Shells are gradually ground into sand by wind and rain.
A bird soars over the crest of a cloud.

Though Father captured the beauty and banality of a mountain village in his album, I sensed a kind of artistic dissatisfaction in the illustrations, as if Father had wanted to give the things in this village something more—a kind of distinctiveness, as of destiny. That nature gives everything a destiny is a commonplace; but in history commonplace destinies—of the buildings of this village, and of the members of this tribe – are quickly forgotten. It isn't that they don't exist, but rather that their existence is silent and shadowy. Father was their only witness. Why, or for whom, did he record their nearly forgotten fates?

Finally I came to Devil's Gulch. I folded pages covered in stories into paper aeroplanes and launched them on a breeze, letting the wind take them where it will. The wind sent those planes deep into the canyon.

Do you like the way I've written our story? I asked.

A gust of wind whined through the valley. I heard a cicada's whistling drone from up ahead. Then I saw a gigantic shadow leap into the canyon.

I am certain it was a shadow, not a cloud. At that moment, I looked up to see the thin beams of a temporarily obscured sun. Then the shadow passed, and there wasn't a trace of cloud. And I'd swear that shadow was shaped like a bear.

I ran to the edge of Devil's Gulch to get a last look at it, but I couldn't see a thing.

This is how I've told the end of Father's story. Father's captioned illustrations end with him leaving the village as a twelve year old boy, but I know the story didn't end there. I didn't have many clues to go on, just a few words and phrases and a couple of sketches.

I go back to my lodging, feeling cold and alone.

I'm the only traveller here.

I open the window; there's just a swathe of barren land outside. By night, it is quiet and still. The only presence is the moon, big and bright. Not a single insect drones. There is not a single nocturnal bird calling in the trees. I can't sleep.

I wander out, following the moonlight, loitering aimlessly, until I hear a sound, faint and fluctuating. I climb up onto a boulder to hear the sound more clearly. The alpine breeze blows gently—the sound is now clear and distinct. A falling leaf flutters across the moon and rides the wind towards the mountain. I decide to go in the direction of the wind, letting it guide me, as in a thousand dreams.

From up ahead comes the sound of a falling twig.

I go towards it, noticing a nest hanging from a swaying branch.

There is another nest nearby. When I come close to it I hear a swishing behind me. I jerk my head to look and see a dark form sliding down another tree. I crouch down in fear, but the shadow runs away. Once I regain my senses, I give chase.

Those ears—I can still see them in the moonlight. Kody! Kody! I am so worked up I cannot speak.

The form seems to hear my silent cry. It stops and looks round at me.

I approach him step by step. He gives a low growl.

I freeze. He comes at me, teeth bared and claws flared. His growl is the same as before, not fierce enough, just a kind of *Oooooo* or *Wuuuuaaaaah.* A few mountain dogs howl in reply.

Kody! I cry silently.

In that instant, he gazes at me, and the wildness in his eyes changes to gentle hesitation. He raises his nose and sniffs the wind.

Several distant bear howls carry through the air. Kody arches his neck up and issues a long cry, as if in answer. His gestures become more agitated.

Kody presses close, with a look of urgent warning in his eyes, a hideous and horrifying expression on his face.

I back up slowly, finally aware that he is a beast, not a human being. He waves his paws in the air, just like a bear.

I stare at him. In his eyes flashes a kind of recognition, a glimmer that soon fades away. He turns and doesn't look back. But I know: we have finally met again, after all these years. That is the most familiar pair of eyes you've ever seen in your life.

Kody is gone.

I go back to the Enchanted Thicket one final time and put the storybook Momo gave me in the hollow in the bat tree. I won't take it with me any more.

Father's face is now blurred in my memory. But occasionally he appears in my dreams. It's always the same scene:

> *A big, bright moon shines on the mountain forest.*
> *A man is hiking alone in the moonlight.*
> *Behind him twirls a leaf.*
> *He places a storybook in the hollow of a tree.*

My father left his mountain home. But he never left childhood. He found permanent lodging in that distant country. I like to imagine him as a boy crouching on the ground in the moonlight, gazing at his shadow. On the head of the shadow he draws a bear's eyes, nose and mouth. Then, gazing steadily at the shadow, he begins to speak…

Valediction

Before leaving the mountains, I paid a visit to the Cataract Cave.

It wasn't winter, but the weather was dry and cold. In Father's album, the waterfall in front of the Cataract Cave was majestically multi-tiered, but in reality it was just a few trickles. There was indeed a cave, but it wasn't covered by a screen of water. When I was there, it was almost completely hidden by rank grass.

When I waded through the grass, I saw a little snake wriggling away. I jumped back and tossed some stones into the clump of grass and the cave. I waited but there wasn't anything there. Finally I got up the courage to go inside.

It was dark and chilly in the cave but not as gloomy as I had imagined based on Father's illustrations. I was amazed by the multitude of glowworms on the ceiling and walls. When I walked close, constellations of faint blue light shone down at me. And then I saw the hollows in the walls—Father's Treasure Troves? I went to see if the collections inside were still intact.

Most of the hollows were full of dust. But one of them was relatively clean—it seemed to have been recently tidied. Something inside caught my eye.

I picked the object up and inspected it.

It was an egg, powdery white with brownish red speckles.

Suddenly I felt tears well up. Maybe, just maybe, there had always been someone to remember:

This one's a red chickadee's egg.

www.ingramcontent.com/pod-product-compliance
Lightning Source LLC
Chambersburg PA
CBHW021018120726
47905CB00009B/3077